Lacey's Retreat

Lacey's Retreat

Lenora Worth

THORNDIKE
CHIVERS

This Large Print edition is published by Thorndike Press®,
Waterville, Maine USA and by BBC Audiobooks, Ltd,
Bath, England.

Published in 2004 in the U.S. by arrangement with
Harlequin Books S.A.

Published in 2004 in the U.K. by arrangement with
Harlequin Enterprises II B.V.

U.S. Hardcover 0-7862-6104-8 (Candlelight)
U.K. Hardcover 1-4056-3084-1 (Chivers Large Print)
U.K. Softcover 1-4056-3085-X (Camden Large Print)

The text of this Large Print edition is unabridged.
Other aspects of the book may vary from the original edition.

Set in 16 pt. Plantin by Myrna S. Raven.

Printed in the United States on permanent paper.

British Library Cataloguing-in-Publication Data available

Library of Congress Cataloging-in-Publication Data

Worth, Lenora.
    Lacey's retreat / Lenora Worth.
      p. cm.
    ISBN 0-7862-6104-8 (lg. print : hc : alk. paper)
    1. Wounds and injuries — Patients — Fiction.   2. New
Orleans (La.) — Fiction.   3. Large type books.
I. Title.
PS3573.O6965L33 2004
  813'.6—dc22   2004042194

To Eve Gaddy, Janet Justiss,
Rosalyn Alsobrook, Denise Daniels
and Sheli Nelson — for the love
and support you have given me as a writer,
and especially for the friendship
that will remain
long after the last words are written.

You are my hiding place;
You will protect me from trouble
and surround me with the
songs of deliverance.
Psalms 32:7

Chapter One

It was just past dawn and the cathedral was quiet and empty.

Lacey Dorsette York sat in the back, enjoying the peace and solitude of the famous St. Louis Cathedral that had been at the heart of the French Quarter in New Orleans for centuries. She liked to come into the cathedral early, just before the morning mass, before the tourists. She liked being alone in prayer.

But this morning even the sanctuary of this old, beautiful cathedral couldn't bring Lacey any peace.

This morning she was finding it hard to pray.

Lacey glanced around, her eyes scanning the colorful murals and frescoes. Painted angels in hues of pink and blue stared down at her with all-seeing eyes. She was alone with the angels. Alone here in this retreat, with depictions of Christ all around — offering to soothe her.

And she needed soothing. She needed to feel close to God this morning.

She'd come to New Orleans to buy some

estate pieces for her shop, The Antique Garden, and to refurbish some of the damaged furnishings her beloved home, Bayou le Jardin, had lost during a flood in the spring.

And maybe she'd come here to get away. Away from the loneliness that seemed to be surrounding her on all sides these days. Her sister, Lorna, now happily married, was going to have a baby early next year. And her brother, Lucas, had just married the woman of his dreams a couple of weeks ago. It had been an eventful summer.

Except for Lacey. She was all alone.

Lacey closed her eyes, tried to form the words to ask God to keep her family safe. Lorna and Mick were in Mississippi visiting some of Mick's long-lost relatives. Lucas and Willa were still in Europe on their honeymoon. And Aunt Hilda had taken a couple of weeks of much-needed rest to visit her friend Cindy up in Shreveport before the two women headed out on an Alaskan cruise.

They'd all had some place to go, something exciting to do, now that the weather was cooler and fall was setting in. So Lacey had volunteered to stay and watch over the badly needed renovations of the bed-and-breakfast antebellum house that provided both their home and their livelihood. While the house was shut down for some landscaping and repair work, Lacey had taken time to get some work done here in the city.

But she wanted to be back in the gardens.

She always missed Bayou le Jardin when she traveled. Especially when she came here to New Orleans, only an hour away. New Orleans reminded her of Neil and what they had shared together. New Orleans reminded her of lost romance and lost dreams. Maybe that was why she'd wound up here in the old church, before she'd even had her first cup of coffee and some beignets at the Café du Monde.

She knew all about lost romance and lost dreams. But her faith had always sustained her. Lacey figured it would get her through this rough spot now, if she'd just hang on and look to God for her answers.

Sitting in the silence, she thought she heard a door creaking open. The cathedral would be filling soon. She'd better hurry. She didn't like the crowds.

Lacey got up, thinking about the tiny grains of resentment she felt toward her brother and sister. They were both happy now. She should be happy for them. And

11

truly, in her heart, she was.

And yet, it hurt. It hurt to know she'd once felt that kind of piercingly sweet happiness, too. Now she felt only a kind of numb pain that never went away. She remembered Lucas's words to her the day he married Willa.

"Maybe it's time for you to come out of hiding."

Maybe.

Lacey again heard a noise up at the front of the big church. Thinking it was probably the priest, she looked up to find a tall, dark-haired man wearing a tuxedo hurrying — stumbling — down the aisle toward her. He had a strange look on his dark, exotic face. A look of hope mixed with pain. He was clutching one hand to his chest, underneath the expensive cut of his evening jacket.

His eyes, so rich and brown, were locked on Lacey.

As he drew near, Lacey's breath caught in her throat. What if he had a gun or a knife? What if . . .

"Help me," he said as he rushed toward her. He looked pale underneath his dark complexion. A fine sheen of sweat beaded just above his full lips.

She jumped up, afraid. But the man was

blocking the aisle. Slowly, her mind on full alert, Lacey sank back down onto the pew. "What do you want?"

"Help me," he said again, his voice deep and ragged. He had a slight foreign accent that seemed more pronounced because of the soft plea.

Then he fell toward Lacey, his eyes never leaving her face. She caught him, her arms reaching up in reaction and protection as he settled across the pew, his upper body landing on her.

Lacey struggled with the weight of him. The warm, masculine-scented weight of him.

With a push and a groan, the man pulled his hand out of his coat front to grab her arm. Shocked, Lacey looked down at his tanned hand, then let out a gasp.

He was bleeding.

"Help me, please," he said again, this time on a raw whisper of pain.

Lacey nodded, too numb to do much more. "I'll get the priest, or maybe the police — let me look outside."

"No!" He grabbed the white lace collar of her cream-colored blouse, smearing it with blood. "No priest. No police. Get me out of here."

She stared down at him. He was lying

across her body, almost in her lap. And his hands still held to the lace at her collar as if it were a silken thread from a lifeline.

"What do you want me to do?" she asked, both afraid and curious. "How . . . how can I get you out of here without being seen?"

He nodded toward one of the side doors leading to the square. "There. Take me through there. First, make sure no one is about —"

He grimaced with pain, then stared up at her again. To her amazement, he managed a beautiful, lopsided smile. "I guess God hasn't given up on me just yet. He has sent me an angel after all."

Then he fainted in her arms.

Lacey didn't move at first. She just held the man there, cradling him as he went limp and still. Then she glanced around, sure someone would come and explain all of this to her, or at least take the bleeding man away. But there was no one.

So she looked back down at the incredibly handsome man in her arms. He was beautiful — dark and lush — like a figure from some long-ago painting of a dark Spanish caballero or vaquero, a fierce warrior. A wounded warrior.

14

But how could she help him?

He'd said no police. That must mean he was in trouble with the law. Did she dare get involved?

Looking down at her ruined blouse, Lacey decided she *was* involved. She'd become involved the minute she'd looked up the aisle and into his eyes.

"So now what do I do?" she whispered as she automatically brought a hand up to check his pulse. He was very much alive. She could feel his breath somewhere in the vicinity of her heart.

"Sir," she said in an urgent whisper. "Sir, please wake up." She shifted, moving his weight.

The man groaned, then opened his eyes. "You're still here, my angel. Not a dream. Not dead." He reached up a finger to her face, touching it with a feather-soft stroke. "Real woman. Pretty, *bonita*." As if amazed, he repeated, "You're still here."

"Yes, I'm still here," Lacey replied in a shaky voice, ignoring the jolt of awareness his touch and his words, both in English and Spanish, provoked. "And thankfully, you're still alive. Can you walk?"

He winced, then tried to push himself up off her lap. Lacey helped him by holding her hands on his arms. "If you can stand, I

15

think I can get you out the door before anyone notices. It's early yet. There should only be a few tourists about. Maybe they'll just think you've had too much to drink."

He stopped her as they stood together. Leaning heavily into her, he said, "Out the side door — the one closest to St. Ann."

"St. Ann?" Lacey had a room in a quaint little secluded hotel at the corner of St. Ann Street and Chartres, across from the Presbytère. She liked staying there because it was close to Royal Street and the cathedral. She could have stayed at her own town house in the Garden District, but that always brought back too many memories of Neil and their time there together. Now she wished she'd done just that. If she had, she wouldn't be standing here holding this wounded man.

He stared over at her, waiting, watching. "St. Ann," he replied. "Can get away, go toward Armstrong Park."

"No," Lacey said at last, wondering at her own logic. "I have a room right around the corner. We'll go in through the courtyard."

He didn't speak. Just stared at her with those intense, burning eyes. "Disguise?" he asked finally.

"What?" It took her a minute to understand what he was asking. "Oh, wait. I have a straw hat." She pulled the crushed hat out of her floral tote bag. "Will this do?"

"A bit dainty, but sufficient." He took the hat with one hand, while leaning heavily on her with the other. Dropping it onto his head, he grinned again. "How do I look?"

"Like a man in a tuxedo wearing a straw hat," she replied. A very good-looking, very hurt man. Dangerous, but irresistible. "Are you ready to go now?"

He managed a nod. "Start walking, angel. We need to hurry. Don't want them to find me just yet."

Glancing around, Lacey was thankful no one had entered for morning mass. She didn't want "them" to find her here with him just yet, either. She only hoped the side door wouldn't be locked. Trying to think, she asked, "Don't you need a doctor?"

He shook his head, pulled the hat low over his brow. That and the shadow of a beard on his square, angular jaw made him look like a bandit. "No doctor. Tiny stab wound from a letter opener. Just a lot of blood." Then he grinned again. "Should see the other guy."

Lacey didn't want to see the other guy. And she didn't want to be involved in a stabbing in the French Quarter, either. And she especially didn't want to aid and abet a man who might be a criminal. If she got arrested or worse, how would she ever explain this to Aunt Hilda? But she was in too thick now to just leave him there, hurt and sick.

Deciding she'd at least get him to her room and get him cleaned up, Lacey went with her gut instincts and slowly walked the man toward the side exit door. She should run away as fast as possible, but something made her stay. Something told her this man wasn't a criminal.

He'd called her an angel. He'd said maybe God hadn't given up on him yet. He'd come to a church for sanctuary.

Or to get away from the crime he'd obviously just committed?

She wouldn't think about all of that right now. Right now she just wanted to get this man somewhere safe. Each heartbeat she felt told her to do that — it wasn't in her nature to leave someone who was suffering — regardless of what that person might be all about.

As they neared the door, they heard footfalls from across the way. The priest coming for morning mass. Soon others would follow.

"Hurry," she told the man. They made it to the door just as the priest glanced up and called, "Can I help you folks?"

Lacey didn't respond. Instead, she pushed at the big door. They came into a hallway, and yet another door. Lacey pushed at this one and felt it open out onto the brightness of early morning. The man seemed to come awake with the glare of the sun. He glanced around, then in a move that caught her off guard, he pulled Lacey away from the door and hurried her past the Presbytère until they were on the corner of St. Ann. He glanced around, his eyes hooded and dangerously alert, before taking a few steps to a gated alcove that looked like an apartment entrance. Then he pulled her close.

"Pretend you're kissing me," he ordered. Before she could protest or push away, he wrapped his arms around her and brought his mouth down on hers, his back to the street, his face hidden by the hat and his body hidden by the building.

Lacey kept her eyes tightly shut as a thousand sensations rippled through her system — the softness of his full lips, the rasp of his unshaven face, the scent of

19

some leftover spicy aftershave, the touch of the sun on her face, the feel of being in a man's arms again. She didn't scream out or move. Then she heard footsteps hurrying by. Angry voices across the street, up near Jackson Square. She knew he was hiding them both — that was it. The kiss was a cover, a desperate act like something out of a silly spy movie.

But it felt like so much more, and brought out feelings she'd forgotten she'd ever had.

The man finally let her go, then looked down into her eyes, a long, hard, misty look, as if analyzing her, as if seeing her in a new light.

Embarrassed, Lacey stole a glance up at him. His eyes were so brown, they seemed like melted chocolate, liquid and on fire. And made *her* feel liquid and on fire, too.

He kept his eyes locked on her for a brief minute, then said, "Look around me, over my shoulder. Tell me what you see."

Lacey ventured a quick glance down the street toward the square. "A few tourists. Some artists and hawkers, a fortune-teller."

"Anyone look strange or out of place? Anyone wearing evening attire?"

"Only you," she said, worry and aggravation coming to the surface to replace some of her awe. "Would you mind telling me what's going on?"

He didn't answer. He just stared up St. Ann, in the other direction, toward a corner grocery store. "I think we're safe now. I think we lost them."

"Them who?" she asked, even as he pulled her back out onto the wide sidewalk. The scents and sounds of early morning in the Quarter assaulted her — coffee laced with chicory brewing, pralines and fresh pastries baking in the restaurant around the corner, leftover trash from the previous evening's revelry leaving a distinctly New Orleans smell — quick and unpleasant for just a brief second. Ignoring these things, she asked again, "Who's following you?"

"Where is your hotel?" he asked, weak but determined as he slowly strolled, holding her hand to make it look as if they were just another couple, while he stayed on full alert.

She noticed he'd managed to hide the bloody spot on the left side of his chest. But there was still blood on his hands, and on her collar.

Quickly, with her free hand, she stuffed the stained lace inside the cotton of her button-up blouse. "Right across the way." She pointed. "We can go through the old carriage entrance, past the lobby. Then up the stairs past the courtyard and swimming pool. My room faces Chartres."

"Secluded, that's good," he said, his gaze darting here and there as they crossed the street.

They made it into the cool darkness of the carriage way. Lacey guided him past the quiet glass-paned lobby door, glad the desk clerk didn't seem to notice them walking by. The courtyard was lush and cool, the ancient crape myrtles and heavy rhododendrons still green in spite of the fall nip in the air. Somewhere in a nearby bush, a mockingbird chirped and fussed. Carefully she took him past the empty pool, then up the back stairs to the second floor.

Within minutes they were at her door. Glancing back at him, she saw that he labored for each breath, and beneath his darkly olive skin a pallor of pain etched his discomfort. He was clutching at his chest again. She found the key card in her leather change purse and with shaking hands managed to open the door while he continued to watch and wait, a look of agony on his face.

Then they were inside the small, quaint room. As he clicked the door shut, Lacey crossed to the French doors leading to a small balcony and quickly pulled the floral-colored drapery shut. The room became instantly darkened.

Taking a long, calming breath, she flipped on a lamp and turned, ready for some questions and answers. Only to find the man sprawled across her bed, her hat crushed in his hand.

He'd passed out again.

Chapter Two

His hair reminded her of black silk. It was straight and clipped, with long bangs around his face and crisp shaggy strands touching on his collar. His eyelashes were shimmering and dark, incredibly thick and lush. His brows were straight, thick and angled, perfectly symmetrical, like a black hawk's wings.

Lacey noticed this as she washed the blood off his face, off his long, tanned fingers. He wore a ruby ring set in intricate silver on his left ring finger, making her wonder if there was someone who was sitting worried about him right this very minute. A wife, maybe? A close female friend?

Well, right now she couldn't concern herself with such thoughts. Right now her only concern was his health and safety. She didn't want him to die here in her room.

She put the rag down to unbutton the tiny studs on his pleated tuxedo front, her gaze following the line of dark hair sprinkled across his broad chest. Taking a calming breath, she managed to get the shirt open without waking him.

The stab wound was just across his left shoulder, dangerously close to his heart. A deep, nasty gash. Just how deep and how nasty she had no idea.

She started to reach for the wet cloth soaking in soapy hot water, but then her gaze caught and locked on something else. A silver rope chain. Lacey touched a hand to the necklace, felt the tug of something heavy. Carefully she pulled the chain away from his right armpit.

It was a cross necklace. A beautiful and obviously expensive antique jeweled cross, heavy and ornate. It was about three inches long, with a brilliant blue topaz in the center, surrounded by lapis and turquoise stones with heavy silver filigree inlay. Unable to stop herself, Lacey reached for the cross, rubbed her fingers over the smooth center stone, held it in her hand.

And felt the weight of his hand wrapping tightly around her wrist.

"Let go," he said, his eyes wild and fevered as he tried to sit up. "Don't take the cross necklace off me."

Stunned, Lacey dropped the cross and pulled her hand away from his. "I'm sorry. I wasn't . . . I wasn't trying to remove it. It's just so lovely."

"It is very old," he told her, his distinctive accent drawing the words out. "Belonged to my *abuela* — my grandmother — passed down through many generations. From my Spanish ancestors."

It didn't surprise her that he had Spanish blood flowing through his veins. His words were laced with that thick, exotic accent. And his skin was olive and dark, his hair thick and rich. His eyes — *ébano* — ebony.

She felt those eyes on her now, questioning, curious, not quite trusting.

"I can see that it's priceless," she told him as she reached for the rag again. "May I clean your wound?"

"*Sí.*" The man tore his gaze from her face long enough to look around the room, as if only now realizing he was in a strange place. "What time is it?"

"Around nine in the morning."

Lacey carefully placed the warm, wet bath cloth over his wound. He winced, but lay back against the white pillow. "A flesh wound," he managed to grit out. "I deflected the blow — he didn't manage to get the knife into my rotten heart after all." He motioned to the cross. "This protected me — it swung across my chest just in time."

Lacey closed her eyes briefly, imagining

26

the scene. Imagining someone coming at him with a knife. He would have leaned away, probably causing the necklace to swing left. Causing the knife to hit the heavy stones, then jab up and over his heart. Just inches away.

"You need a doctor," she said. "You need stitches, a shot against infection, something."

"I have everything I need," he said, his hand coming up to still hers, his dark eyes rising to her face. "Just wash it and stop the bleeding, *por favor.*"

"It's slowed down some," she said, very much aware of his warm hand on her cold one. "I found some bandages in my overnight bag — I always get blisters when I walk around New Orleans in this humidity, no matter how cool the weather, nor how comfortable my shoes." He tried to sit up, but she pushed him back down, hoping her prattling would calm him. "You need to lie still for a while."

"Until dark," he responded, his hand still on hers. "Then I have to go."

Lacey swallowed back the fear and some other unnamed emotion rolling through her system. How would she be able to stay here with him all day? *Should* she stay here with him all day? "Where are you going?"

"You don't need to know that, angel."

Lacey lifted the rag, then pushed his hand away. "Look, I don't know how you got this wound, or why you asked me for help, but the least you can do is explain yourself. I think I deserve that much, at least."

The man looked up at her, his intense gaze scanning her face. "You kissed me."

That was not the answer she had expected. "No, *you* kissed me."

"But you didn't seem to mind very much."

"I didn't have a choice. You *forced* me to cooperate."

He gave her that beguiling grin again. "No, you cooperated rather nicely." His gaze fell across her mouth. "Very nicely."

"You're delirious. *You* kissed me to hide your face, to hide from those men who were running through the Quarter."

He lifted one dark swooping brow. "Did I?"

"Yes, you did," she replied hotly, amazed that he would tease her about this. "And I don't see why. I mean, you could have just turned your back from the street and . . . those men . . . whoever they were. You didn't have to be so dramatic, did you?"

"It was an impulse," he replied. "But

28

very pleasurable, considering the circumstances. I don't regret it. Do you?"

She blushed. She felt the heat moving up her neck all the way to her hairline. Jumping up, she said, "Never mind how I feel. Do you always act on your impulses? Is that what got you hurt and on the run?"

"Probably," he replied, his face, his eyes as dark and shuttered as the room. *"Lo siento."*

Lacey said a silent thanks for the Spanish lessons Aunt Hilda had insisted they all take in high school. She was rusty, but at least she could communicate with him. After opening the large square bandage she'd found in her small cosmetics bag, she placed it across his wound. "Too late for sorry. Are you going to tell me . . . anything?"

"No. *Nada.*"

He closed his eyes, as if he were taking a nice nap. But she could see the hard line of his jaw, the tiny beat of a pulse that told her he was very much aware of her and his surroundings.

"I want some answers," Lacey said. She threw the rag back into the ice bucket she'd used to bring hot water to the bedside.

With his eyes still shut, he said, "The

less said the better, angel. I don't want you to get hurt."

"How thoughtful of you." After handing him a glass of water and two pain pills, Lacey moved away from the bed and went into the bathroom to wash the blood out of the once white bath cloth. "Too late to worry about that, too. I'm involved," she called out. "You know that, don't you? You got me involved, so you need to tell me what we should do next."

She came out of the bathroom, stared down at the bed where he lay. His eyes were still shut, and he had one hand turned up across his forehead. The other hand was clutching the cross medallion.

Lacey swallowed, took a breath, said a prayer. The most beautiful man she'd ever seen in her life was lying in the middle of her four-poster hotel bed, in the middle of the French Quarter, with a knife wound to his chest.

And he was clutching a cross medallion.

All of this before she'd even had breakfast.

Suddenly Lacey didn't feel so lost and alone anymore.

Now she just felt utterly confused and disoriented, but very much alive and aware.

Because whether this man gave her answers or not, she knew deep inside that her life was about to change, that she'd made some unspoken agreement with this stranger.

To help him. To become even more involved with him.

All she could do now was wait and watch, and pray that she wasn't making a huge mistake by following her instincts and her heart. And her heart wouldn't allow her to leave anyone hurt and abandoned.

"Can you at least tell me your name?" she asked, her voice calm in spite of her runaway pulse.

"Gavin," he said. Then he fell asleep again.

He woke up alone.

Well, that was certainly nothing new.

Gavin looked around the darkened room, wondering for a minute where he was and why he was here. Then he remembered.

"*Haló*," he said, his voice raspy, his throat as dry as sagebrush. "Angel, are you here?"

He wouldn't blame her for running. She should run.

And yet, he wanted her here.

He pushed himself up off the bed, saw the stark white of a note on the nightstand.

"Gavin, I've gone to get us something to eat. I'll be back soon. Lacey."

Her name was Lacey.

It suited her. She was all feminine and soft, all lace and light, with her golden-blond hair and brilliant blue eyes. She smelled like a thousand flowers, and her face was so breathtaking, it had beckoned him back from a familiar darkness.

That darkness had surrounded his soul as he'd fled into the night, leaving behind the life he'd always known, leaving behind any remnants of innocence and happiness. He knew the truth now, the horrible truth.

Maybe that was why he'd wound up inside the church. To hide from the truth, to find some sort of peace in the midst of all the turmoil, all the pain, of betrayal.

Gavin winced as he tried to sit up. Shadows fell across the quiet room like the layers of a sheer veil. It must be getting late. He glanced at the pretty clock on the table. Almost five. Darkness would fall soon. Then he'd have to leave.

He'd have to leave Lacey.

That would be for the best. He felt rested now, better. Some food would be good. That would help him, give him strength. And he'd need every ounce of strength he possessed to get to the bottom of this mess. He needed time to think, to figure out his next move. To plan.

Someone wanted him dead. And he now knew the reason.

Sitting there, Gavin touched a hand to the cross.

All he had to do now was find that someone, so Gavin could clear his own name, clear up this trouble. It would be ugly, nasty work. He might not make it through. But he was determined to stay alive. Thanks to his grandmother, he had a strong faith, in spite of the darkness swirling up around him. He held to the cross and closed his eyes. He would survive.

And maybe . . . when this was all over, he'd come back to New Orleans and he'd find Lacey again.

But first, of course, he had to get out of this room. He had to get away from the Quarter.

He got up and made it into the bathroom. He took off his shirt, then stood there studying the flesh-colored bandage Lacey had put across the cut. He could see bloodstains pooling against the dressing.

"Well, Gav, you've really messed up this time, *tonto*. Now what?"

Not finding any answers in his reflection, Gavin bent to splash cold water on his face and head. Pain sliced through his left shoulder, but at least he wasn't dizzy or weak anymore. The pills and the rest had helped. And as soon as he had some food in him —

Then he straightened, reality hitting him harder than the cold, icy water. "Lacey?"

She'd gone out alone to get food. What if someone had seen them together? What if someone had been watching, waiting for them to make a move?

Panic set in. Gavin whirled, grabbed his shirt. What had he been thinking, involving an innocent woman in his troubles? Why had he asked her for help? Right now, this very minute, they might have her somewhere. And Gavin knew exactly what these people were capable of doing.

His heart cut at his chest, threatening to burst through his very skin. He had to find her.

He was struggling with his shirt when the door opened and she walked inside, like a breath of spring, to stand there staring at him with those wide deep blue eyes.

Gavin didn't even realize he'd let out a long sigh until he heard her voice.

"Are you all right?"

He managed to nod as he leaned over, his hands propped on his thighs. "You . . . you shouldn't have gone out alone."

She lifted her chin in a beautifully stubborn defiance. "I was hungry and I'm having major caffeine withdrawals. Thanks to you, I never got breakfast."

"A little late for that, don't you think?" he replied, mirroring her earlier words to him.

She brought the bag of food over to a side table. "Yes, it's now dinnertime and I'm still hungry. I sat here all day long, worried about you, afraid to leave you. But then, you seemed to be resting soundly, so I decided it would be all right to go to the restaurant around the corner. I got us some po-boys and coffee. With cookies for dessert. And I bought you a new shirt and a hat of your own." She tossed him a light blue cotton T-shirt and a dark baseball hat with a sports emblem emblazoned across its front. "Do you feel like eating?"

"I could use the coffee," he replied as he dropped into a chair beside the table to remove his stained shirt and carefully replace it with the soft cotton one. It was a slow process because of his injury, but he couldn't help but smile at Lacey. She turned away while he changed, every bit the lady. The beautiful, blushing lady.

"*Gracias,*" he said finally, allowing her to turn back around. Then he stared across at her. "Did you see anyone? Anybody follow you?"

"I watched my back," she replied as she ripped the lid off one of the plastic cups of coffee. "And I changed clothes and wore my hat."

"Smart lady." He took a bite of the fried crawfish po-boy. The spicy food hit his empty stomach with a fiery explosion. He was still jittery from worrying about her. Grabbing the hat, he plopped it on his head, just to have something to do. "Are you sure no one followed you back here?"

"Pretty sure," she said, frustration coloring the words. "It's crowded out there. No one bothered noticing me."

Gavin thought that was a false statement if he'd ever heard one. She was tall, cool and blond. Hat or no hat, men would notice a woman like . . . his Lacey. And she was cultured and ladylike in her lace and flowing floral skirts — not something one often saw in the Quarter on a late Friday afternoon.

He watched as she broke off tiny pieces of French bread from her own turkey sandwich. She obviously came from money, old money. Gavin knew all about old money. He knew it was much cleaner than new money — the kind hidden away in secret locations.

Putting thoughts of treachery out of his mind for now, he tipped his hat low over his eyes so he could study Lacey instead. Her clothes, her mannerisms, everything about her was class, right down to the way she held her napkin on her lap and took measured chews of her food. Dainty. Feminine. Pretty.

And completely out of his league.

"This is good," he said finally, needing to fill the silence that moved between them. "Thanks again."

She fidgeted, got up to turn on the television. "Maybe we can watch a movie until time . . ." She stopped, looked around at him as the evening news blared out behind her. "Until what, Gavin? What are you planning to do next?"

Gavin was just about to answer her when a familiar face flashed across the broadcast. Lacey watched his face, saw his sudden interest, then followed his gaze as she glanced around at the television screen.

Then she spoke. "That's Senator Prescott. They're investigating him for some sort of scandal — something to do with payoffs from some of the casino people."

"*Sí*, I know who he is," Gavin said, his heart thumping a stark warning against his chest.

Lacey turned back to the television, her eyes scanning the screen. "My Aunt Hilda says the casinos are the root of all evil. But . . . they did bring in jobs and help the economy."

"If you say so." He wondered who Aunt Hilda was, and he wondered if Lacey knew just how much evil there was out there on those streets. Suddenly he wanted to protect her, to keep her safe right here for a very long time.

But it wasn't going to be that easy.

Lacey shot him a quizzical look, then once again glanced at the television. "They might indict him. At least, the evidence is leaning that way." She was about to turn the channel when another face came up on the screen. Letting out a gasp, she watched the screen, then glared at Gavin.

Gavin hissed a breath as he looked at his own image plastered there for all the world to see. For Lacey to see.

Lacey didn't speak. Instead, she sank back down on her chair, the remote control still in her hand.

Thankfully, it was an old picture — one from his college days. He looked young and alive, nothing like the way he looked today. He'd probably aged fifty years since then.

The anchorman told the rest of the tale.

"And to complicate matters even more, Senator Prescott's son, Gavin, is reported to be missing and is now wanted for questioning. The news came after an elaborate dinner party at the senator's New Orleans home last night. Apparently his son got in a scuffle with another guest, but left the residence before security or the police could question him. It is believed that Gavin Prescott might be hiding important information about his father's alleged dealings with the head of the gambling cartel that owns La Casa de Oro Casino. The House of Gold, as the locals call it, opened up with much fanfare last year as the first land-based casino in New Orleans. Shortly after the successful opening, however, an investigation into Senator Prescott's finances was launched. The FBI wiretapped his home and found incriminating evidence that the cartel, owned and operated by the powerful Currito family, had bribed the senator to help get a gambling license. This launched a full-blown investigation into the senator's holdings. The Currito family insists the senator coerced them into payoffs, but the senator declares he is innocent. His son, a member of his father's impressive team of lawyers, has now apparently become a suspect himself. More on this fascinating story at ten."

Lacey turned off the television, then slowly shifted to face Gavin. "You're *that* Gavin — Gavin Prescott, as in *Senator Edward Prescott?*"

He could only nod. Then he managed to set the record straight. "*Adopted* son. My mother married him after my *real* father died — when I was five years old."

If she heard the venom in those words, she ignored it. Good. He really didn't want to explain things, especially the hostile relationship he'd always had with his so-called adoptive father.

She let that soak in, then said, "I should have recognized you. I mean, this is a big story. It's on the news almost every night. I'm sure since you're a lawyer for your father's defense, I must have seen your face before on television or in the papers."

The shock in her voice made the words

40

whisper thin. Those words tore at Gavin's heart.

"I haven't been a prominent part of the proceedings," he finally said. "More like a silent spectator — kept in the background." *Kept in the dark.* He tried to stifle the bitterness, but it was there in each word he spoke.

Lacey must have picked up on it. "The news said you got in a fight at a party. Did something happen between the senator and you last night?"

"You could say that."

"And now, obviously, that's why you're on the run." She stood then and placed both her hands on the table between them. "I think we need to talk, Gavin. I think you need to tell me exactly what happened and why you're in hiding. And I'd really like to know what I'm supposed to do about it."

Gavin reached out a hand, wrapping his fingers around her slender wrist. "I want to explain everything, *querida*. And soon I will, I promise."

Lacey pulled her wrist away. "No, right now. I have to know what I'm up against. I'm expected back home in a day or so. I have to go . . . but I don't want to leave you if you need help."

Gavin sighed, placed his elbows on the

table, then yanked off the hat to bury his head in his cupped hands before lifting his face to her. "If you can just help me to get out of the Quarter. There's somewhere I have to go. I have to find out the truth, before it's too late."

She stared down at him, her blue eyes reminding him of azure waters, distant and swirling. "You're in a lot of trouble, aren't you?"

"Yes."

And then Gavin heard it. Just a bump and a thump against the outside wall of the room, near the locked door. He peered at the slant of skinny sun rays coming through the narrow crack at the bottom of the door. And saw a shadow cutting through the western sun. Other guests coming up the stairs, or somebody else?

He got up slowly, pressed a finger to his lips, then motioned toward the balcony. Not wanting to take any chances, he put the hat back on, then pulled Lacey close in his arms and said, "We have to leave. Now."

Lacey looked around. "Why?"

"Because someone is just outside the door. And I think they are about to be inside this room."

A hard rapping on the door indicated he was right.

Wide-eyed, Lacey grabbed her tote bag, clutching it to her chest as if it would protect her. "Should we answer that?" she said, her voice low, her eyes wide with fear.

"No way. We're going for the balcony," Gavin told her as he took her by the arm and eased her across the room.

Outside, he could hear the shuffling, the footsteps hovering. Then he heard voices, speaking low. Another loud knock. "Management. Sorry to disturb you, but we need to talk to you for just a minute."

He shook his head at Lacey, then placed a finger to his mouth to keep her quiet. "When we get outside and over the balcony, I want you to run, Lacey. Run as fast as you can."

"Over the balcony? You can't make it over the balcony."

"Yes, I can. You just do as I say."

"What about you?"

"I'll be right behind you. Trust me."

Gavin only prayed that she would trust him. Because it might be the only way he could keep her alive.

Chapter Three

Lacey kept telling herself this wasn't really happening to her. Things such as this didn't happen to a nice woman from the country. She was a widow in her early thirties; she led a dull, boring, but contented life at Bayou le Jardin. She went to church each Sunday and served on various committees during the week. She had a nice, efficient business to keep her occupied, work that she enjoyed. She wasn't the type of person to climb over a balcony in the French Quarter and run through the dusk with a handsome, mysterious wounded man, while two other men were bursting through the door of a hotel room even as they made their escape.

And yet, she was doing just that.

She could hear the door creaking open. Could still see the determined effort in Gavin's eyes as he'd flung her through the French doors, and told her to jump from the intricate wrought-iron balcony railing to the street. They'd barely made it to the shadowed catwalk beneath the second-floor overhang before the two men had come running out onto the tiny balcony.

And she didn't dare look back to see if the men were chasing them. But she thought she heard frustrated shouts coming from the hotel.

"My car is in the parking garage," she told Gavin through winded breaths as they rounded the corner of Dumaine Street, heading for Decatur. "We could get it."

"No. That would be the first place they'd look for us," he told her through gritted teeth.

Lacey held his hand. He hadn't let her go since they'd climbed halfway down a woven iron balustrade and dropped the eight feet or so from the balcony. But by the twisted grimace on his face she could tell he was in pain. And she could see the little spot of blood from his wound coming through the cotton of his shirt. But he kept running, and he kept pulling her right along with him, both of them holding on to their hats.

Glad she was wearing cushioned sandals, Lacey huffed, "Then where are we going?"

Stopping for a minute to catch his breath, Gavin tugged her behind a towering magnolia tree. "We're going to have to circle back around, get out of the Quarter. Then I need to get out of New Orleans for a while."

45

Not stopping to think about what that meant, Lacey said, "I have a town house in the Garden District. It's secluded, back away from the street. If we could make it there —"

"We'll do it," Gavin said. "Just for tonight. I need to think, make some phone calls."

"Are you sure that's wise?"

"I have a couple of people I know I can trust."

He looked down at her then. The moonlight cascaded over his features like a soft spotlight, making him look both sinister and sad. "Do you believe I'm innocent, Lacey?"

Her heart raced as she tried to find breath. "Since I'm not really sure of what they're accusing you, I can't answer that." She stood there looking at him for a minute, then said, "But I think you are definitely in trouble. And you're hurt. I'll help you get to a safe place, at least."

He tilted his head down. "You could have run in the other direction once we left that room. Why didn't you?"

She didn't quite know the answer to that question herself. "I was so scared, I had no choice but to follow you."

"I didn't mean to get you so involved,"

he said, his hand touching her windblown hair. "Don't worry about me, *querida*. After tonight, I promise you won't have to deal with any of this again. I'll be out of your life by sunrise."

That promise should have brought Lacey relief, but for some reason it only made her feel empty and lost. And even more worried. But she didn't have time to think about that now. Gavin was tugging her through the darkness again.

"Stay close to the buildings," he advised. "If anyone comes by, we'll just act like we're out on a date — two tourists strolling through the Quarter."

"Except this isn't exactly the safest part of the Quarter," she whispered.

He nodded. "We'll get back around to Decatur, blend in with the crowds, then go to Canal and Carondelet to catch the streetcar back to the Garden District. Where is your town house?"

"Just off St. Charles on Felicity."

They rounded the corner toward Decatur, merging with the crowds waiting in front of Jackson Square for carriage rides, then doubled back to St. Louis, heading toward Bourbon. Lacey could hear the revelry from here. Aunt Hilda would not approve, but what choice did she have? Of course, Aunt Hilda wouldn't approve of her hiding a hurt man in her hotel room all day, then running away with that same man who was being chased by some scary people, either.

Get a grip, Lacey, she silently told herself. After all, she *was* over thirty. Perfectly capable of making her own decisions, however impulsive or crazy they might seem.

Only, she had never been impulsive or crazy. She'd always left those two traits up to her lovable siblings, Lorna and Lucas. Lacey was supposed to be the calm, sane Dorsette. Mentally shaking her head at her own folly, she glanced over at her traveling companion.

He looked completely in control. Alert and calculating, silent and still. A stranger guiding her through a maze of mystery and intrigue.

So much for being sane. Lacey did the only thing she could do in such a situation. She prayed. Hard. And while she prayed, she pushed back the memories that had stayed with her since childhood — the memories of running through the night with Lorna and Lucas, the memories of voices shouting in the dark. The memories of watching her missionary parents being executed by angry rebels deep in the heart of Africa.

Gunshots. Rain. Screams. Lacey held off the memories, sending them to that safe, secret place in her heart. She had to stay calm, just as she'd stayed calm that night. She had to. So she kept on praying.

Gavin did a quick surveillance of the area, and apparently satisfied that they weren't being followed, pulled her toward the crowds. He also tugged her close, his left arm slung over her shoulder in spite of his pain.

Lacey didn't pull away. She felt safe clutched close to him like this. He kept her in the shadows, tucked against the buildings. He watched each face they passed, his whole body alert in spite of the smile on his face and the lazy way he clung to her. Every now and then he dipped his head toward her, as if to caress her face.

It helped ease her fears, helped keep the harsh memories at bay. She could almost believe they were just a couple out on a date. Almost.

But then she remembered that her day had started out on a strange twist and things had gone downhill from there.

"They'll be looking for us in the crowds," Gavin told her. "Let's take a left on Conti, then switch back to the right on Royal. We can go through Exchange Alley from there and make it to Canal."

Lacey hurriedly followed him, in spite of her winded state. She was afraid to let him out of her sight now.

"You certainly know your way around New Orleans," she said as they neared Exchange, her nerves as tight and quivering as the guitar strings of the lone musician who stood on a corner, playing for tips. The song was slow and poignant, but the chords and notes rose out over the night on a sweet melody.

"I've lived here all of my life," Gavin told her.

"But not on this side of town, I gather."

"No, angel. My . . . the senator has a big house uptown. When I was a teenager, I used to escape through a window and roam the Vieux Carré at night."

"You were a bad boy, then?"

He pulled her onto the narrow strip of Exchange Alley, his gaze falling across her face with a purposeful intention. "I still am."

Lacey swallowed as a warning shiver moved like tapping fingers down her spine. She breathed deeply, hoping to find air in the cool night breeze. She had so many questions. "Gavin, was that really the hotel management, do you think? Or was it the police looking for us, or maybe Currito's people?"

"You catch on quick, I see," he said, one hand on her shoulder. "I don't think it was management. In a quaint hotel such as that one, they would have addressed you by name, since the room is registered to you. And in normal circumstances, the police would have to announce themselves, but . . . this corruption runs deep. For all I know, it could have been some of Currito's men posing as management or the police. They did knock, though, just before they managed to open the door, of course. They were probably hoping to gain entry, then make their move."

Lacey shivered again. "I've heard things — the Currito family is very powerful. Some say they are the local Spanish Mafia. If they sent someone after you —"

He touched a finger to her lips. "Hush. Don't think about it. I won't let them get near you." Then he glanced around before adding, "But I don't think the Currito family sent them. They are trying very hard to run a clean operation, from what I hear. I think the senator sent them."

She let that soak in, understanding that

these people, whoever they were, would hound Gavin if they thought he had information that could hurt them. But had they tried to kill him? "*Do* you know something about your father's dealings, something that could incriminate him?"

He looked down at her then, his dark eyes shining like a midnight moon. "What I know I can't say right now, Lacey. You are better off *not* knowing." Then he dropped his hand away. "We need to get moving."

They hurried up Exchange toward Canal, past the restaurants tucked away in the short alley. Gavin scanned the street before they walked out onto Canal. "It's pretty crowded. I think we're safe. Let's keep a low profile while we wait for the streetcar."

They headed up Canal, then ducked into a corner store, waiting there until they could hop a ride to Lacey's town house. Lacey didn't ask any more questions. But just as soon as she got Gavin to the town house, she intended to get to the bottom of this.

It occurred to Lacey as she unlocked the door that she hadn't thought of Neil very much today. But she was thinking of him now.

She didn't like being here. Rarely came back here. Even though Neil's family lived in Florida now, they had given the tiny two-story cottage to Lacey and Neil as a wedding present, and had insisted Lacey keep it after Neil's death. Mimi Babineaux, a cousin to the Babineaux clan back at Bayou le Jardin, kept the place clean and restocked with essentials, in case any of the Dorsettes did come to the city. Lucas had brought Willa here a few months ago, during her visit with the doctors in New Orleans.

It was like a haven, tucked away from the main street, surrounded by towering oaks and magnolia trees, tall, thick azalea bushes and clusters of banana plants. From the street it looked like a carriage house or detached garage, but the tiny secluded courtyard centered in the back made it completely private. Which was why Lucas always referred to it as Lacey's retreat. But it wasn't a retreat to Lacey.

Now a whole new set of memories assaulted her as they entered the French doors just off the long, narrow kitchen. Memories of her time with Neil. They'd had their honeymoon right here in this house. Then later she'd come here to sit alone with Neil's child growing in her, while she still mourned her husband's death.

And then later, memories of nothing. No child. No husband. Nothing left in her life. Both husband and child were now buried in the tiny family cemetery back at Bayou le Jardin, near the Chapel in the Garden.

Maybe because she was scared, confused and tired, maybe because a great grief tempered with a tremendous guilt weighed at her soul, Lacey felt her emotions brewing over like a cup of hot black coffee. Scalding emotions that would soon have her crying. And she couldn't let Gavin see that.

But he must have sensed it. "What's wrong, *bella?*"

She turned to face him. He stood just inside the doorway, his masculine presence filling the room with a darkly macho strength. An overpowering strength that didn't really fit in here amid the clutter of chintz-covered furniture and delicate Victorian lace. But in spite of the aura of danger surrounding him, his eyes held traces of fatigue . . . and concern.

"You're tired," he said before she could find her voice. "I've dragged you all over the city. Why don't you get a bath, get cleaned up. Rest."

She shook her head. "I need to tend to your wound. You're bleeding again. Why don't *you* get a hot shower while I see what I can find for us to eat. How about some coffee?"

He nodded, his expression still puzzled. "It's a lovely house, Lacey."

"Thank you."

"So, you live in New Orleans? Why were you staying at the hotel, then?"

"No, this is just a second home. I . . . I live about an hour from here, on a very old plantation. It's a bed-and-breakfast. Bayou le Jardin."

He came closer, placed a hand on one of the tiled white counters. "*Sí*, I've heard of it. You get tourists?"

She turned to busy herself with making the coffee. "Yes, but earlier this year we had a terrible tornado. It ruined the village and did a lot of damage to our property. We're closed right now, during the slow season, for repairs. I came to New Orleans to do some antique shopping, to replace some of the pieces we lost to a flood right after the tornado."

"A flood and a tornado. Sounds as if you needed a vacation."

She smiled then. "Yes, I did. But you, sir, are certainly no vacation."

He bowed with a gallant flourish. "I do apologize. I wish we could have met under different circumstances."

"Me, too." Then she pushed a hand through her hair. "Let me take you upstairs to the bathroom. And . . . I'll get you some clothes. You're about the same size as my husband. There's still a few of his clothes around here somewhere. They should fit."

After she said it, she stopped, holding her breath because of the shocked look on Gavin's face. And because of the nonchalant way she'd just offered up her husband's treasured garments to a stranger.

Gavin let out a long breath. "You're . . . married?"

"Was," she managed to say, her voice just above a whisper. "My husband died about five years ago."

"I'm sorry." He stood there, his head dipped low, those black brows lifting toward her. "You're still grieving."

"Yes." She had to look away. The tears pooled in her eyes, making it hard to see the bright red light on the coffeepot. "I suppose I will always be grieving. It's the kind of pain that just never really goes away." Then she shrugged. "We . . . we celebrated our honeymoon here in this little house. It's always hard, coming back — that's why I stayed at the hotel instead."

"You loved him."

She turned to face Gavin then, saw the awe and admiration in his eyes. And she saw something else there, too. Something she recognized easily, since she'd been suffering the very same emotion in recent weeks. Envy. But it wasn't the jealous kind of envy. It went deeper than that. Gavin envied her the love she'd once had, just as she now envied her brother and sister the love they had at last found.

"I did love him," she said, knowing she had to be completely honest with Gavin — this man who stirred her soul in ways she didn't even want to begin to explore. "I still do."

He came toward her then, placed his hands on her arms. "I have never known that kind of love," he said, his gaze sweeping over her face with a hunger that took her breath away. "But I tell you this, Lacey. Your husband was one lucky man. To have loved a woman like you. One very lucky man." Then he touched a finger to her nose, his eyes filling with regret. "I'll have that shower now."

Gavin stood underneath the hot mist,

wondering if maybe he shouldn't have a cold shower instead of a steaming one. To cool off the treacherous thoughts running through his head, to temper the yearnings moving like a river through his tired system.

"You can't have her," he told himself in both English and Spanish. And yet, he wanted her. He wanted to get to know her, to make her smile and laugh, to wipe away that sadness he'd witnessed on her face the minute she'd walked into this untouched dollhouse. Her pain was so deep, she preferred staying in a hotel to being here again.

He'd forced her to come back here, to a place that obviously held many wonderful memories for her, in spite of the pain. A place where she had lived and loved and known all the things he would never know. All the things he could never give a woman.

Frustrated, Gavin got out of the shower and toweled off, then went into the tiny bedroom where Lacey had left him some clothes. A pair of jeans and a button-down cotton shirt lay across the quilted comforter. Her husband's clothes. Would it hurt her to see another man wearing them?

"I did love him," she'd said. "I still do."

"Not a good situation, Gavino," he told

himself as he dressed, feeling strange and out of sorts by being in both the clothes and this house.

He had to get away from here, and soon. He wouldn't put Lacey through any more danger. She was a good woman. Too good for the likes of him.

But first he had to make a phone call. Gavin had to ask the question that had been burning through his brain since last night when the bodyguard had attacked him right outside his father's back door. Had tried to kill him right there in his own home.

And he knew exactly the person who would be able to answer his burning question.

His life had changed over the past twenty-four hours. Had gone from bad to worse. He combed his hair, then closed his eyes, his fingers straying to the cross medallion. Gavin wished he could go back, back to the time when he was blissfully ignorant. Back to the time before he'd found out the harsh truth.

But he could never go back now.

"But one good thing did come of all of this," he said out loud as he held the comforting weight of the jeweled cross in his hand.

Lacey.

The most beautiful woman he'd ever seen was waiting for him downstairs. Too bad he'd have to leave her in the morning, to protect her, to save himself. And too bad she was still in love with another man.

Chapter Four

Lacey watched Gavin's face as the news report flashed yet another picture of him across the screen. Sitting there in Neil's old clothes, Gavin looked every bit as handsome as he had last night when he'd come down after his shower. But seeing him in her husband's clothes had definitely brought Lacey out of her awestruck stupor. She'd dashed off to get her own bath, then pleaded tiredness before going off to her own bedroom. Now they were having breakfast together, a perfectly normal ritual on most days.

Of course, this wasn't a normal day. As the morning news indicated with precise, clinical details.

"Still missing and still wanted for questioning, Gavin Prescott, the son of Senator Edward Prescott, is said to allegedly have information regarding the investigation of his powerful father. Did Senator Prescott solicit bribes from the Currito family in exchange for helping them obtain a gambling license in Louisiana? And does his own son know more about this case than anybody? More on this developing story tonight at five."

"That's a very good question," Gavin said as he clicked off the small television set sitting on Lacey's kitchen counter. Then he looked across at her. "And probably one you'd like me to answer."

Lacey saw the earnest expression on his haggard face there in the morning sun. He didn't look as if he'd slept very much last night. Well, she certainly hadn't, either. She was worried about so many things. What if her family heard about this? Of course, they had no way of knowing she was on the lam with a man wanted for questioning in a high-profile court case. Then she'd worried about her actions, about everything that had taken place in her life over the past twenty-four hours.

And yet, she knew in her heart she'd done the right thing in sheltering Gavin. Somehow, she just knew. She kept remembering the way he'd clutched his cross necklace.

And she kept remembering the way he'd kissed her.

Wondering how she instinctively knew that Gavin was innocent in all of this, she glanced down to the cross he was still wearing. She reckoned he'd slept in the heavy piece of jewelry. The image that provoked caused her to suck in her breath and say a quick prayer for more pure thoughts.

"Why don't you tell me everything," she suggested as she brought the coffeepot over to warm up his brew. "How did your phone calls go last night?"

"I had a long talk with a man I know I can count on — used to work for my father. He's looking into some things for me." Gavin shrugged, then grabbed another piece of French toast with his fork. "Surprisingly, I couldn't reach my mother. She is the one other person I feel I can trust in this, and her cell phone should be secure for now. But she didn't answer last night."

"Surely she's worried about you," Lacey said as she slipped into the chair across from him. She ignored the little tremor of pleasure his presence across from her provoked. It was just good to have someone, anyone, here in this house with her. She reminded herself that this particular someone was a hunted man, on the run from things she probably didn't want to know about.

"*Sí*, I'm sure she's worried," Gavin said, his eyes guarded. "But . . . you'd have to know my . . . father. He demands complete respect and loyalty."

"So she has to be careful?"

"Yes, very careful. I'm going to try her again this morning. She will be away from the house. Today is her spa day, I'm sure."

Lacey nodded. She'd seen Nita Prescott's picture now and again in the society section of the *Times Picayune*. Nita was a beautiful woman, dark and exotic, much like her son. And extremely wealthy, thanks to her powerful husband. But how a mother could traipse off to the spa when her only son was in serious trouble was beyond Lacey. It didn't make much sense. "Do you think you can really trust your mother?"

He shrugged again, gave her a cool, blank look. "At this point, I'm not actually sure if I can completely trust anyone." His expression seemed to change as his gaze moved over her face, however. "Except you, of course."

"So what are you going to do?"

"Hide for a while. I need access to a computer. I think I know where all the records are located, but they're buried underneath certain codes. I can get to them, but it will take time and extreme measures. I was so close the other night —"

"You were snooping in your father's files? Is that why you got hurt?"

He gave her a soft, cynical smile. "That's right, *bella*. I found out something the other night that made it all fall into place, but before I could find the rest of the proof to back up my suspicions, my father sent a henchman to take care of me — or to scare me, at least."

Shocked, Lacey sank back against her chair. "Your father? So you really think your own father wants you dead — had someone try to kill you?"

"My *adoptive* father," he reminded her with a bitterness that was hard to miss. "But yes, that's exactly what I think. The man had a gun, but I managed to knock *that* out of his hand. *Estúpido,* I didn't think to grab the letter opener before he did. And even now I can't be sure if he was Currito's man or my father's. He's been working for my father, but who knows."

"Tell me everything, Gavin," Lacey said, shivering at the horrible scene forming in her mind. "If you want me to help you, you have to tell me." When he didn't respond, she said, "You said you trust me. And right now I'm your only hope."

He nodded, took a long sip of coffee. Then he pushed his plate aside and leaned forward, careful to favor his sore left shoulder. "I'll tell you just enough to make you understand how serious this is. Someone wants me dead, because they think I've found out the truth, the whole truth."

"Which is?"

He shook his head, his dark spiked hair falling across his forehead. "Which is something you don't need to hear."

At her frustrated groan, he added, "Look, Lacey, I shouldn't have involved you in this in the first place. If they find me here —"

"They won't."

"If they do, you could be in danger." He reached across the table then, taking her hand in his. His skin was calloused and rough in places, and soft and warm in others. "Yesterday I purposely hid in the cathedral, just so I could stop and think, get my head clear. I was there when you came in." He stopped, gave her a long, measured look. "I waited for you to go, but you just sat there. I knew others would be coming soon for early mass. And I also knew some of them might be trouble, men looking for me. So . . ."

She held to his hand. "So you came to me to get *me* out of there?"

He ran a hand over his hair. "I don't know, maybe. Or maybe I just wanted a closer look at you. You see, I had been lying there on a pew, looking up. I wanted to pray, but . . . I think I'd forgotten how. Then I saw an inscription in Latin. *Te Deum Laudamus, Te Dominum, Confitemeu.*"

Lacey repeated the words in English. "We praise thee, O God. We acknowledge thee to be the Lord."

"Yes," he said, smiling. "My Latin isn't the best, but I managed to decipher the words enough that I began repeating that inside my head." He stopped, his eyes holding hers. "And then I saw you."

Lacey felt a heated rush of emotion pouring over her. "So you thought —"

"I thought I'd better take advantage of the situation, test the theory that maybe God was trying to help me."

"You called me an angel."

"You looked like one sitting there."

Lacey took a deep breath. "But I didn't do anything very angelic."

"You got me out of there," Gavin said, his fingers moving over her hand, stroking her skin, making her shiver in spite of the warm sun nearby. "If I hadn't found the strength to go to you and ask for help, I feel certain I would have passed out right there and . . . the priest or whoever found me would have called the police."

"And you'd be in even greater danger."

"Exactly. As I said, my father is very powerful. He has so many people, from beat cops to detectives and on up the line, in his pocket. He pays them well. Enough that they'd have no qualms about bringing in his renegade son."

"On trumped-up charges?"

"Unfortunately, yes. And that's what I'm up against. The records I cracked last night had been altered to make me look bad, but I know the real ones are buried deep inside a computer's hard drive or possibly copied onto a disk somewhere. If I don't find those records, they'll twist this around to make it look as if I'm the guilty one. If they can pin the bribery and corruption on me instead of him — which is exactly what it looked like when I stumbled into the files last night — I'll take the fall for all of them, right up to the Currito family."

"Do you have proof that the senator bribed them?"

"I was working on that when my friend with weapons came to pay a visit. I can't prove it was all my father's doing, or if the Currito family offered him a bribe. But I will. I have to. The senator was so angry with me, he fired me — told me I was disinherited and out of a job. Then I guess he decided to get even before the FBI could get to me. I have to clear my name and get these goons off my back."

"So what do we do next?"

He let go of her hand then. "You — you're going to go home to the bayou, *querida*. And you're going to stay there and forget you ever met me."

She wondered if she'd ever be able to forget a man like Gavin Prescott. "Just like that?"

"Just like that, or as soon as I can sneak you out of New Orleans."

The phone rang then, causing Lacey to jump, causing Gavin to scowl. "Be careful," he said as she went to answer it. "Don't give away anything."

"Hello?" Lacey held the receiver with a white-knuckled grip. "Yes. Yes, I understand. I had an emergency and I'm so sorry — I just forgot — yes, thank you."

She hung up then to face Gavin. "That was the hotel, supposedly. They found some of my things in the room. They think I accidentally left them — just a change of clothes and some small purchases, and probably your bloody clothes where I tossed them in a laundry bag. Since I had express checkout, they didn't question me

69

— just said they'd send them to my house."

Gavin nodded. "Do they have the address to Bayou le Jardin?"

"Yes, the hotel does, but —"

His eyes went on full alert then. "But what?"

"Gavin, the hotel doesn't have *this* number. No one but my family and Mimi, our cleaning lady, has this number or this address."

"Are you sure? Are you sure you didn't give it to the front desk?"

She shook her head. "They have my license plate number, of course, and my car is still there, but I paid for parking through today, so that shouldn't really matter. I don't give this address out to anyone — there's never been any reason to do so. Whoever that was — I don't think it could have been the hotel."

He hissed a breath, then looked around, out the open door to the secluded courtyard. "Lacey, we have to leave. Now."

"You think it was —"

"I know," he said as he pulled her toward the door with him. "They tracked us down and they were checking to make sure they had it right."

Lacey tugged away long enough to grab

her faithful tote bag off the back of a chair, then she hurried to turn off the coffeepot, practicality winning out over fear for the moment. "So they know I'm here. That doesn't mean —"

He turned then, grabbing both her arms, his dark eyes bright with anger and impatience. "It means they have your name and this phone number and they have an address. And it means they are on their way here. And Lacey, if they find us — if they find you here with me, it could be bad. Very bad."

"Okay. Okay." She pulled away from him again, checking her bag to make sure she had her cell phone and other pertinent information. Then she glanced around, her gaze scanning the small room for anything that might lead their stalkers to Bayou le Jardin. Fortunately, she didn't keep any important papers or any vital information here, since she rarely came here.

"I don't think there is anything here for them," she said. Because she didn't dare think about what "very bad" could mean for her, she busied herself with mundane things such as tossing their few breakfast dishes into the sink, then running water over them.

Groaning, Gavin shut off the spigot and

whirled her around. "Lacey, this is serious. We have to leave right now. Forget all of this. It won't matter anyway if something happens to you."

She could see the fear — fear for her safety — in his dark eyes. "I understand," she managed to say as he propelled her out the door. "I hate leaving this mess for Mimi, but I guess I don't really have a choice." Then she pivoted back to the door. "At least let me lock up." She turned to fumble with the bolt on the French doors.

Gavin's wry chuckle hit the morning air. "Locks won't keep them out, Lacey. And as for the mess — when they get through with this place, I'm afraid dirty dishes won't matter very much."

She locked the door anyway, as a means of protest against this senseless invasion of her home and life. She'd hate to see her precious things destroyed, but then, she stayed away from this place on purpose. What did it matter now? "You're right, of course. And I certainly don't want Mimi to walk in on them. I'll call her and tell her she doesn't need to come by today."

"And what explanation will you give her?" Gavin asked in a low voice as he edged them toward the gate.

Lacey let out a frustrated sigh. "I'll tell her I got called away unexpectedly, an emergency back home, and she can just come by later in the week to clean the breakfast dishes. I don't know, I'll think of something." Then she turned to face Gavin, a defiant streak coloring her words. "Well, let's go."

"But where, that's the question." He shoved a hand through his hair as he carefully looked both ways up and down the long alley. "I need to think —"

Lacey stopped, glanced around at him as they silently opened the gate. "I have an idea, Gavin."

"I'm open for suggestions," he said, guarding her with his body while he made sure no one was lurking in the banana fronds near the back alleyway.

Lacey let out the words on a rush of breath, not sure why she was doing this. "We can sneak back to the hotel and get my car. Then we can go to Bayou le Jardin."

Gavin sent her a surprised look. "Bad idea. They had your things — they might be waiting for us to show up back at the hotel. And they might find us at Bayou le Jardin, too."

"But they didn't verify *that* address over

73

the phone," she explained. "They were going to send my things *here,* to this address, which is why I knew it couldn't be the hotel, since the hotel doesn't even know about this place. It could have just been another trick, but even if they do know about Bayou le Jardin, they won't find us there. We can hide out in the swamp."

He shot her an incredulous look. "The swamp. I don't really do swamps, *bella.*"

"I grew up there," Lacey said as they hurried out the gate and down the narrow, tree-shaded alley. "And my brother, Lucas, can take us so far back into the bayou no one will ever find us. He should be home in a couple of days."

She hoped.

Gavin opened his mouth to say something, to object probably, but the words died on his lips as he craned his neck to stare at something just past Lacey. "Run," he told Lacey, the expression on his face startled but determined.

Lacey heard a low piercing sound, then felt the whiz of a bullet passing right by her head. They were using guns with silencers! She didn't bother arguing with Gavin anymore. And she surely didn't bother looking back. But she could hear footsteps running close behind them.

"Lacey, listen," Gavin said as he hurled her along in front of him at breakneck speed, dodging and ducking between trees, cars and fences. "Keep running until we can find another alley, then veer off as fast as you can. Maybe we can hide in one of these big yards, then make our way back to a more crowded area."

Another round of bullets pinged off a nearby metal storage shed.

"We've got to get out of here." Gavin grabbed her hand, his eyes locked with hers and they took off down the alley. They were once again running for their lives.

Chapter Five

They whirled around a giant crape myrtle tree, causing dry crusting pink blossoms to shower them as they passed into a driveway between two gingerbread-style mansions. Gavin grabbed Lacey and pulled her into a backyard, behind a tall white fence that served to camouflage two big black trash cans. Sinking to his knees, he crouched down, then yanked Lacey down with him. "Stay low," he whispered as he peered through the slits of the wooden fence.

"I think we might have lost them somewhere between the two Mercedes and that SUV parked back there," he said between great huffs of air. "They turned off in another direction, thanks to that barking dog." Watching to make sure they weren't being followed, he sighed long and hard. "One of them was my friend from the other night — a big fellow named Randall, I think. He can't run very fast, but he can sure pack a punch." He heaved another breath, then leaned back against the fence and closed his eyes. They'd managed to dart in and out between cars and houses enough to confuse the big thugs, but he knew the henchmen would find them again. Those kind always did. "And he's a pretty good shot." Touching a hand to Lacey's disheveled hair, he asked, "Are you okay? The bullet didn't graze you anywhere?"

Lacey shook her head, sucking in much-needed air. "I'm fine, but that was a little too close for comfort."

Gavin tugged her down so they could sit with their backs pressed against the fence. The big trash cans hid them from the alleyway, and he had a good view of the wide yard and street in front of them.

After scanning the entire area, he relaxed a little, his hands lying loosely across his bent knees, then looked over at Lacey. She was a trouper, hanging on to that ridiculous floral bag as she ran, but he could see the sheer fright in her eyes. She'd probably never been through anything so violent and unnerving in her life. "Let's just sit tight for a couple of minutes. Make sure they aren't still on the trail." Just to lighten things, he added, "We can always hide in the garbage cans, I suppose."

Lacey wrinkled her nose in distaste. "Even rank garbage is preferable to the alternative."

Gavin's heart lurched at her words. She could have been shot, killed, back there. He wished for the thousandth time that he'd never forced her into this with him, but now that she was here, it was up to him to protect her. Somehow. And that meant getting her out of New Orleans.

Once again looking around, he considered stealing a car, but decided he didn't need to add that crime to his growing list of mistakes. The only choice was to walk out of here and find a way out of the city.

The day was humid in spite of fall settling in all around them. The giant oaks and magnolias were shedding some of their leaves, causing rustling sounds that set Gavin's already wired nerves on edge. One of the lovely mansions was decorated with a life-size scarecrow sitting on a hay bale guarding two bright orange pumpkins. It should have been a pleasant, comforting sight. Somehow, given the circumstances, it looked ominous to Gavin.

"It seems as if I've done this before," Lacey said out of the blue. Then she looked straight into Gavin's eyes, and he saw something in the azure blue of her gaze, something that made her seem vulnerable and almost childlike. Something

78

that tugged painfully at all of his protective instincts.

"Oh, really?" he asked, trying to understand what that look meant. "I can't imagine you running from killers, sugar."

Her nod was slow, her eyes still on his. "When I was twelve, we were living in Africa. My parents were missionaries. They were murdered by some rebels. They came in the night and . . . I can still remember hearing the sounds — the gunshots, my father screaming at us to run, run away." She stopped, breathed deeply. Gavin felt her beginning to shake. "We had to hide underneath a round, thatched hut — we called it the round house. My parents used it as a church."

Her eyes, so blue they looked like a vast, deep ocean, grew bright with memories. And tears.

"Ahora bien," Gavin said, pulling her close to stop her shaking. "Now then, *querida*. It's all right. It's all right. How horrible for you. How awful."

She clung to him there in the grass and shrubs, hidden behind the trash cans. And Gavin cursed himself for putting her in this position. "I'm so sorry, so sorry. I will get you safely back home, Lacey. I promise."

"I'm okay," she said, but her teeth seemed to be chattering in spite of the sun shining down on them. "I guess this brought it all back." She tried to pull away, tried to straighten her hair. "Funny, I did okay when I saw the blood on your shirt yesterday. I even held it together when those men burst into our hotel room. But today — I suppose it was being back here, back at the town house. It just triggered so many memories. But I'm okay, honestly."

Gavin held her there, knowing that she wasn't okay, honestly, knowing she had a beautiful instilled sense of pride. She'd probably never had a chance to fully mourn the death of her parents, or her husband, either, for that matter. She hid her inner suffering behind a serene wall of domestication and ladylike classiness. But inside, she was hurting. Just like everybody else — just like him.

Their chance encounter had brought it all crashing back — for both of them. But he didn't want to make things any worse for Lacey.

"I have to get you back home," he said, stroking her hair as he rocked her against him. "Lacey, can you hear me? Do you understand — I didn't know, darling. I didn't

80

know you'd been through something so tragic."

"We don't talk about it very much," she said on a whisper. "Lorna was afraid of the dark. But now she has Mick and she's doing so much better. She's going to have a baby." Her eyes grew wistful and sad, in spite of her smile.

Gavin closed his eyes and wondered why God allowed someone so beautiful and loving to experience such a tragedy in her life. And how she'd managed to find even more trouble by associating with the likes of him — whether by chance or by fate. "Do you want to talk about it?"

Lacey lifted her head. "Not really, but it's there as always, staring me in the face. Lucas is married now, too. He was so reckless before, so daring. Now he has something to live for. He's . . . settled now."

"That's good, *querida*, that's good."

"Yes, I keep telling myself to be happy for them. But . . . the other day in the cathedral, even while I thanked God for their happiness, I also prayed that He'd take away my sadness. It was more of a resentment, really. I just wondered why . . . why I'd had so much happiness once, and then it was all gone. All gone. And you see, I still have so much love to give, so much in-

81

side me that sometimes I just want to burst with it. So much . . . and no one with whom to share it. Sitting there in the cathedral, I'd never felt so all alone." She looked away, out over the spacious, sun-dappled garden. "I was having one big pity party, right there by myself. And then you came along."

Something liquid and hot bubbled inside Gavin's soul, something both intimate and unfamiliar at the same time. He didn't know how to respond to such honesty, wasn't used to seeing someone's emotions so close-up and crystal clear. "And then I came along," he repeated with regret. "And now your life is in total chaos."

"But I'm not *alone*," she said simply, softly.

"Lacey —"

She looked up at him then, as if realizing where they were and why they were here. "We should go."

"Lacey?"

"I'm okay. Just a temporary lapse of reason. I just got a little shaken back there." She was silent for a while, but she fidgeted with the sturdy beige canvas straps of her ever-faithful Monet-inspired water lily tote bag. "This is real, isn't it, Gavin?"

"*Sí,* very real. But I won't put you in any more danger."

She touched a hand to his face then, taking away his breath and his resolve. "Don't you see, we need each other now. They know who I am. They've seen my face."

Gavin put his hand over hers. "You're right. And because of that, I am responsible for your safety. Which is why I'm sending you home. Alone."

Her eyes grew bright again. This time with determination. "No. You're coming with me to Bayou le Jardin."

He shook his head, agitation making his accent thick. "I don't think that is so wise, Lacey. I can hide away without your help. Believe me, when I was younger I knew how to disappear very easily whenever I wanted."

But Lacey's sensible practicality was back in full force, apparently just as effective at shutting out her emotions as the wall at their backs had been at shutting out the world around them for a brief time. "You're coming with me, Gavin. If we stick together, I can help you to clear your name. We've got everything you need — computers, phones and a place to hide."

The honest trust he saw in her eyes

caused those funny sensations in his chest again. He didn't deserve her trust, surely didn't deserve such a woman, but just knowing that someone believed in him gave him such a feeling of hope, and brought him such humility, that he hated to give up. Finally he let out a long sigh. "Well, we can't sit here all day, that's for sure. And . . . if I keep you close, at least I'll know you're safe."

"And I can protect you, too," she said, a wry smile edging her full pink lips.

"Oh, and how is that?"

She touched a finger to his cross necklace. "I can pray for you."

Then she got up, dusted her skirt off and offered him her hand.

Gavin took it, still amazed at the rush of protective feelings pooling deep inside the dark recesses of his heart.

Lacey was right; he couldn't let her go. Not only because he wanted to protect her, but also because he wanted to be near her. Just near her. It was wrong of him to feel this way, but he did have his own rare moments of complete honesty, too. And yet, he couldn't be honest with Lacey. He still had so many secrets to guard.

It was like walking on a tightrope.

He took her hand, looked around to

make sure no one had spotted them, then tugged her through the canopy of trees and shrubbery to the busy thoroughfare of St. Charles Avenue.

"We should be there by nightfall," Lacey said a few hours later. She was driving him away from the city.

She was taking him to her home.

In her car.

"I still can't believe we managed to sneak back and get my car," she said now, as if mirroring his own thoughts.

"You're one brave lady," Gavin said, his head back against the leather headrest of her late-model sedan.

"Well, as you said, it makes sense they're no longer watching the hotel. And management — the real hotel management — knows I left suddenly by now. I had to get my car, or risk even more explaining."

"Yeah, or having it towed and getting the police involved, which is something we need to avoid."

She nodded, maneuvered around a curve in the narrow country road. "I think my disguise worked okay, don't you?"

Gavin had to chuckle in spite of the tension coiling in his neck muscles. He still couldn't believe he'd let her talk him into retrieving her car from the parking garage back at the hotel. But it was either that or take a taxi all the way to Bayou le Jardin, or steal some other means of transportation. In the end, the simple logic of Lacey's argument had won out. The people after him would probably be looking elsewhere by now, and she had just enough time to get the car before the hotel became suspicious and had it carted away.

He'd agreed to this plan only after they'd watched the hotel parking garage themselves for about an hour, and only after Gavin felt sure no one was waiting there for them.

Since St. Ann was on the fringes of the Quarter, it had just been a matter of getting the car and hightailing it back to the Interstate, once they were sure they weren't being followed, of course. All in all, not a bad plan.

He was beginning to see that about Lacey, though. When she didn't want to deal with those dark memories, she went to work. She fussed and fidgeted, she calculated and planned. She stayed busy. Gavin could just picture her in her quaint antique shop, dusting and rearranging, changing and shifting, a perfect picture of primness and business. And all the while, she was lonely and hurting, her pain locked safely away behind that tranquil demeanor and that practical attitude. Now she had a new cause to keep her occupied; she was obviously out to save him, both physically and spiritually.

He didn't have the heart to tell her he was a lost cause.

He glanced over at her now. Gavin supposed if he had to be on the run, at least he'd had the good sense to pick a smart woman to help him. "You know, with the short black wig and that . . . interesting dress, no one could mistake you for the very ladylike Lacey York."

"I'm going to toss the wig," she replied, grimacing down at the offending black clump of hair in the seat between them, "but I just might keep the dress."

"I can't argue with that," Gavin said, his eyes sliding over the short black knit sheath she'd hastily bought at a boutique on St. Charles. "You look very —"

"Un-Lacey-like?" She grinned over at him.

And caused his heart to turn to something close to bayou fen, mushy and unpredictably soft. "I'm glad you can find humor in all of this," he said. Then he added, "And I like you whether you're very

Lacey-like or very un-Lacey-like."

She smiled again. "We don't know much about each other, really, do we?"

Gavin shook his head. "No, and if I told you everything about me, you'd stop this car and kick me out onto the levee."

"I highly doubt that. But I do have a question."

He lifted his brows, giving her a sideways glance. "Oh, here we go."

"No, seriously. You are obviously very much of Spanish descent. So . . . why is your name so very American?"

He leaned back against the soft leather again, his eyes on the winding stretch of road that followed the Mississippi River. "My real name is Gavino Colon — Salvador Colon was my father's name. He brought my mother to America when they were just married, and he found work here in New Orleans, thanks to some family connections. But he died way too young, of a heart attack, when I was five years old."

"Then your mother married Senator Prescott?"

"Yes. They met at a fund-raising event — she was working as an interpreter for a government official, and he was an up-and-coming city councilman. After they married, he went on to run for higher offices. He finally made it to the state senate. Anyway, right after they got married, he adopted me out of the goodness of his heart."

Lacey gave him a sideways look. "You don't like him very much, do you?"

"No, I guess I don't. He made my mother change my name to Gavin. Said a more American name would protect me. He just couldn't handle my Hispanic heritage, I think. He didn't seem impressed that both my mother and my father were descended from Spanish aristocracy — noble but impoverished at this point, I'm afraid."

"And yet he adopted you."

"Only to control me, I assure you."

"But you can't be controlled?"

"Apparently not, or I wouldn't be in this mess."

"You worked for him."

"Yes, I felt I owed him after he put me through law school at Tulane and insisted I become a junior partner in his executive law firm — corporate law at its finest."

"Do you like corporate law?"

"I did." He stopped, glanced out at the fall foliage passing them by. "I wanted to be the best. In spite of my hostility toward my adopted father, I wanted to gain his respect. I think I always wanted that. But instead, I became his lackey. I was supposed to jump whenever he said jump."

Holding a hand to his nose, Gavin pinched his nostrils to ward off the headache forming. "I just got tired of trying to please him, tired of trying to second-guess him. And then I got suspicious. Too much money was changing hands, and I was expected to make sure it all got to the right places. I felt like a water boy, always carrying something. Yet whenever I'd question him, he'd turn things around to make me sound ungrateful or paranoid."

"So you think he *has* done something illegal?"

Gavin wagged a finger toward her. "No, no. We are going to stop with this line of questions, right now. I've already said way too much."

"Well, I need to know what we're up against."

"Not we, but *me*, Lacey. I'm up against a lot of things. You — you just need to stay clear of things. I accepted your help only because I feel obligated to protect you and watch your back, but that doesn't mean I have to fill you in on all the details."

"You don't trust me completely, do you, Gavin?"

"Yes, I trust you. But I'm not going to tell you things that could harm you."

Her cheerful mood whirled away with the passing countryside. "Then how am I supposed to help you?"

Gavin saw the stubborn set of her lovely jaw. "Only on a need-to-know basis."

"I see."

She turned silent as the car rounded a curve in the road. Gavin glanced back, as he'd done all the way from New Orleans, to make sure no one was following them. The long winding road was empty and flat. He turned back around, then sat up straight at the sight spread out before him. "Is this your *casa?*"

"Yes," she said on a quiet breath. "This is Bayou le Jardin."

Gavin swallowed once, then took in the majesty of the pink-hued mansion with the wraparound galleries and huge Doric columns sitting back behind a long row of lush evergreen live oaks. "It's beautiful, Lacey."

She nodded, her blue eyes misty with pride. "And you know what they say, Gavin? *Mi casa es su casa.* Or words to that effect."

Gavin understood what she was saying.

And he also understood that by agreeing

91

to come here, he'd taken a very dangerous step. Dangerous for Lacey's well-being.

But perhaps even more dangerous for his own hurting heart.

Chapter Six

"This could be dangerous," Gavin told her for the tenth time since they'd turned on the computer in the office just off the kitchen. "We're talking the cops, the FBI and the Currito gang, not to mention the nasty people who work for the senator. If they trace anything back —"

"I'm trusting you to cover your tracks," Lacey replied as she handed him a glass of iced tea. "You seem to know what you're doing."

He nodded, took a long sip of the tea. "Yes, I'm hacking into my father's computer system. One of my many admirable qualities."

"How did you learn . . . to do this?"

"You mean, perform criminal activities without batting an eye?" His mouth lifted in a half smile. "Remember when I told you how I'd sneak out at night and roam the city? Well, sometimes I got caught. Papa Prescott's idea of punishment was to put me under house arrest. I was confined to my suite of rooms, with one of his personal bodyguards to watch over me. The fellow knew a lot about technical crimes and computer espionage, so to speak. Harry Crane — that was his name. He was there right in the middle of the beginnings of the information superhighway, knew everything there was to know about the Internet. He was bored being assigned to a teenager, so he taught me everything he knew before he moved on to a more dignified way of making a living at a legitimate software company. Meanwhile, based on what he'd taught me, I spent a lot of time at my computer, playing games and exploring new technology."

She smiled at him. "So you were a computer nerd?"

Gavin nodded, grinning. "A lawyer and a computer nerd. A very bad combination, huh?" Then he stopped grinning. "I never knew both would come in handy in defending my own life."

Lacey was beginning to understand the estranged relationship between Gavin and his father. "Sounds as if this Harry spent more time with you than the senator did. I can't believe you were held prisoner in your own home."

Gavin scowled even harder. "And now it seems I'm being held prisoner in yet another form. If he catches me, I can assure you he will gladly lock me up again — with trumped-up evidence for the FBI. But this time I'm not a child. I learned to fight dirty out on the streets, and I will do whatever it takes to bring him to justice. He's controlled my mother — and me, too — for way too long. It took me so long to see the truth, to finally put all the pieces together, but this time he won't get away with it."

Lacey sat down on the floral divan next to the desk. She could see the grim determination in Gavin's eyes as he went back to his work. She saw no fear there, no qualms about what he had to do. Gavin seemed to possess a great sense of justice, of knowing right from wrong, in spite of the trouble and intrigue all around him.

She wondered how he'd managed to retain that kind of integrity, what with roaming the streets of New Orleans and having a corrupt father for a role model. Then she glanced down at the beautiful cross necklace he wore. That piece of jewelry meant something to Gavin. Maybe it represented his own kind of faith, too.

Lacey wanted him to win, wanted him to find validation. She didn't yet understand why this was so important to her. She just knew in her soul that Gavin was on the right side of the law and that goodness always prevailed over evil.

So she quieted and sank back in her seat. "Go on about your business. I'll just read or something."

"Read, yes, that would be wise," Gavin told her through a wry smile. "Best you don't see how I'm getting in through the back door here."

But she didn't want to read. She wanted to watch Gavin. He was such a fascinating man. He was obviously very smart, brilliant. He was a lawyer with a degree from Tulane, but from what she could gather from their conversations, his talents had been wasted working for Senator Prescott. He also seemed to be a technological whiz, from the way he keyed in computer codes and watched files and data flash across the screen.

And . . . he was so beautiful.

So dark, so very different from Neil.

She kept thinking of Neil, guilt and grief filling her heart. Neil had been blond and athletic, all spit-shined and clipped to military precision. Neil had always taken her breath away. She had loved him with a devotion that swelled with sweetness and light.

Gavin Prescott wasn't sweetness and

light. He was darkness and danger. And yet, Lacey couldn't stop herself from remembering the way he'd kissed her that morning in the Quarter. Nor could she forget the way he'd clutched his priceless medallion, his amulet, in his hands as he'd stared up at her with those jagged ebony eyes.

Was she doing this because she wanted to help him? Or was she doing this because she was so very drawn to him? Was there so little excitement in her life that she was willing to get herself involved with an obviously dangerous man? Or did she just want something to keep her busy, to keep her mind occupied so she didn't have to face another empty day?

He needs someone, she told herself now as she watched his eyes scanning the information on the screen. He needs someone, and he found me.

So here they sat at midnight in the quiet darkness of the great old house. No one was around for miles, and because of recent rains, the construction workers and extra groundsmen they'd hired wouldn't be back for a couple of days. But Lacey wasn't afraid or fearful. She again felt a kind of inner sense, an instinct that told her she was doing the right thing. She felt safe with Gavin.

As she watched Gavin, she thought about this afternoon, when she'd brought him here to her home just as the sun was setting over the river. After parking the car and making sure nobody was about, they'd walked up the path to the house, then she'd given Gavin a tour of the old mansion.

"The parlor and dining room," she said, standing in the middle of the marble-floored central hallway, her arms arcing to both sides. "And behind the stairs in back, two bedrooms that we rent out when we're open for business. On the other side, the kitchen and our private den and office, which used to be a butler's pantry — we have our main computer in there. The Babineaux family usually hangs out in the office, but we gave them and our landscaper, Justin Hayes, a much-needed vacation this week."

She moved around the house, describing antiques, telling him the names of the stoic ancestors staring down at them from gilt-framed portraits. "We had to replace some of the flooring down here, because of the flood. And we've ordered some new rugs, actually old rugs — Aubusson and Turkish carpets — to replace the ones we lost. We managed to put some of the furniture up on blocks before the flood hit, so that helped salvage some of the oldest pieces."

She'd talked nervously but quietly as she guided him through the rooms, very much aware that she was alone with him.

"Your parents?" he asked, pointing to the portrait over the mantel in the front parlor.

"Yes."

"You look very much like your mother."

Lacey smiled at that. "Thank you. My mother was a lovely woman. Her name was Elisha. Elisha and Parker Dorsette. Everyone called my father Park because it means cypress tree in Chinese — Aunt Hilda found that out on her many travels and started calling him that when he was very young. But in fact, Parker means keeper of the park. He loved the swamps and bayous, loved being out in the gardens."

"They look happy," Gavin said. "It's a nice picture. I'm sorry you lost them."

"Thanks. It's been rough at times. But they were doing what they loved, what they felt called to do. And they're with God now."

Gavin nodded. "But you have good memories."

Lacey touched a hand to the gilt frame.

"Mostly. Except for the horrible way they had to die. You know, Lorna held on to this picture when she got trapped here during the flood. The electricity went out, and she was terrified — she's been scared of the dark since the night they died. She said the picture helped her to feel safe in the darkness. So I do believe they were here with her that night."

Gavin had touched a hand to his necklace, his fingers unconsciously rubbing the brilliant blue topaz center as he studied the portrait. "They watch over all of you."

"Yes, I think they do."

Now Lacey wondered if Gavin's real father watched over him. They had that in common, the loss of a parent. That kind of loss ran deep and colored everything, each aspect of a child's life. Lacey knew her parents' deaths had certainly set the course for her family. She was only just now beginning to understand how deeply her own grief had affected her. Then she remembered — once she'd been happy, she'd overcome that initial grief. Neil had made her whole again. But her happiness had been fleeting and short-lived.

Now, in spite of her deep, abiding faith, Lacey could see she'd been only half-alive, half-worshipful, and that her attempts at understanding were mired in a deep and sad resentment.

She should thank Gavin for making her see that she'd only been floating through a hazy existence. Finding him, bringing him here, had made her see that being alive was a very important blessing. One she should never take for granted.

So she watched him as he worked by the light of a single lamp, and she wondered about this stranger, this dangerous stranger, who'd literally fallen into her lap. She wondered if this was all a part of God's plan, a part of His divine intervention. Had God sent Gavin to force Lacey out of her self-imposed seclusion? Or had she just become mixed up in something she'd only regret?

Gavin stopped typing and looked over at her, startling her out of her musings. "Why are you staring at me, *querida?*"

She lifted her head. "Was I staring? I'm sorry. I guess I'm just amazed by you. You play that computer like a piano."

"Nothing amazing about me, I can assure you," he said, his words rasping out on the still air like a fencer's dancing sword. Stretching, he grimaced as his wound protested the sudden movement.

"Are you in pain?" she asked. "I could

get you some aspirin. We probably need to change that bandage and put some more of Rosie Lee's ointment on it."

"I'm fine," Gavin replied, a shadowy smile on his dark features. "You should go to bed. It's late."

"I'm . . . not sleepy," she admitted. "It's strange, being here alone. I'm used to having my family all around."

"And not used to having someone you barely know in the house with you." He swiveled in the chair, his dark eyes glowing with a question. "Do I frighten you, Lacey?"

"Of course not." Not in the way he thought, at least. The most frightening thing about being around Gavin was the way he made her feel. Alive and humming. Aware and alert. On guard, but guileless. And very guilty.

She got up then, her need to fidget overcoming her need to watch him. "We could take a midnight stroll through the gardens. It's nice and cool out."

He arched a dark brow. "That might relieve some of this tension in my shoulders. And some of the tension I can see in you." Then he hit another key. "Let me just save this information on a disk."

"Did you find what you were looking for?"

"Not yet. It's all there, but I've just got to fit it together. The paper trail is long and wide. A bank statement here, a document there. The senator keeps meticulous records, but he has covered his tracks very well. Obviously he's paid his accountants very well, too." His voice held a bitter, hard edge. "And he managed to hide it all from me, right under my nose. Which really makes me angry, considering he always assured me I was his most trusted confidant."

"You've been betrayed," Lacey said. "That has to be an awful feeling."

Gavin shut down the computer, then got up to face her. "Sometimes I feel as if my whole life has been one big betrayal, beginning with my real father's death."

"Well, right now you can put all of that aside. Aunt Hilda says we can carry our troubles to the garden and God will be there waiting."

From the dubious expression on his shadowy face, it was clear Gavin doubted those words. Lacey wanted to prove him wrong. So she took his hand, led him out onto the gallery.

The night was still and calm, brisk with just a hint of autumn. She could smell the earthy aroma of the orange and burgundy colorful mums. Justin had planted the beautiful flowers around the property before he'd left to embark on yet another gardening tour somewhere up in New England, where the leaves were beginning to change colors. A full moon set a misty gray cast over the trees and flowers, and thousands of stars twinkled like fireflies above their heads. Nearby, an ancient camellia bush flourished with bright pink fluffy blossoms.

"Lovely," Gavin said, his voice just above a whisper.

Lacey turned to smile at him, thinking he was referring to the gardens and the fall night. "Yes, the four seasons are always beautiful here."

"I wasn't talking about the weather," Gavin said.

Her smile died on her face. Gavin was looking at her with such a sweet intensity, it made her dizzy. She couldn't speak. Couldn't move. Her skin felt clammy in spite of the crisp, cool night.

He stepped close, took one of her hands in his. "Moonlight becomes you, *bonita.*"

She lowered her head, touched a nervous hand to her pearls. "Thank you."

Gavin brought a finger to her chin, forcing her to look up at him. "I told you this could be dangerous."

Misunderstanding, she shook her head. "Don't you feel safe here, away from the city?"

He chuckled. "From the killers, *sí*. But I don't feel so safe around you, Lacey."

"You have nothing to fear from me," she replied, but her heart tripped up over the words even as she said them. Hadn't she just thought the very same about him? There were many kinds of dangers in this world, she realized. And many kinds of deceptions. She wanted to be honest with Gavin. "I'm just here to help you, Gavin. Not scare you."

"But I think you do scare me," he replied, his dark eyes shining like gemstones. "I've not had easy relationships with women. I've hurt people. I've been ruthless, dogged in trying to do my job. And because of that, I've always guarded my heart — no time for distractions, you understand. But I think my heart is in a very dangerous place right now. If I do become distracted, you could very easily break it."

"Don't be silly. I've never been known as a heartbreaker." She managed a feeble smile, willed her own heart to stop dancing. "You're safe here with me, Gavin. I don't have any illusions about things. I don't expect . . . anything from you."

His hand moved over her hair. "That's good. I don't want you to have any illusions. I can't —"

"You can't make any promises," she said, finishing his words for him. "And I don't expect any promises. The plan is to clear your name, keep these crazies from finding you, right?" She tried to move away then, because she refused to think past the obvious, refused to give in to any treacherous thoughts or needs. Or illusions. "So what do we do next?"

He tugged her back around, his hands pulling through her hair. "Forget promises. How about this?"

He touched his mouth to hers in a kiss as soft as a dew-covered blossom, a caress as fresh and exhilarating as the wind in the tall oaks. Then he lifted his head. "No promises, Lacey. And yet, I wish I could promise you the moon and the stars."

She touched a hand to his jaw. "Right now I think I can settle for another kiss."

He shouldn't have kissed her, Gavin thought hours later as he stood at the open French doors of the first-floor bedroom.

It was a lovely room, complete with a huge cherry-wood bed and a matching armoire and dresser. The furnishings were old and cozy and polished to a high sheen that glistened against the night. He felt as if he'd stepped back in time. How he wished he could do just that.

Unable to sleep, he looked out over the dark gardens. The moonlight and wind made the shadows dance and frolic, and made Gavin paranoid and too alert. So he stood watch, edgy and restless, while upstairs on the third floor, Lacey slept.

He wondered how she slept. Did she wear that enticing strand of pearls to bed? Did she sleep in lace and silk, perfumed lotion on her smooth, soft skin? While she lay there alone in her bed did she dream of her husband and the life they'd had together?

Stop it, Gavin told himself. Stop thinking about a woman you can't have. Stop thinking about the way she kissed you, the way she sighed in your arms. Stop thinking about the way she makes your cold, bruised heart pump with life and hope again. "It can't be, Gavino," he told himself.

And yet, since he couldn't sleep, and since he was so close to figuring things out, but still getting nowhere with the senator's shady dealings, he resorted to a sweet dream. The dream involved Lacey, in her pearls and satin, with her arms opened to him. It involved Lacey pulling his head down to hers, her lips meeting his. It involved laughter and smiles and happy, sunny days. And beautiful, lovely nights.

"Stop it," he said out loud.

He thought about leaving, just sneaking out into the night. He could go underground; he had friends on the streets of New Orleans, friends who, while they weren't the most noble of folks, would be willing to help him out.

In spite of his mother's protests, he'd done some pro bono work on the side, just to keep his sanity. Because he'd always been fair, and he'd always worked for the underdog, he'd gained a certain notoriety among the wretched souls of the streets. Now he was the underdog. They'd help him, hide him, do whatever he asked them to do.

And then Lacey would be safe. She'd be away from him and his unrealistic dreams. She could go back to her civilized, calm, good life. Being alone was much better for her than being with him, after all.

He almost did it. He almost headed out the door. Then he remembered if he left her here, she would indeed be alone. And very vulnerable. If the senator or the Currito gang found out anything, anything at all, about Lacey and how she'd helped him, she'd be a sitting duck for revenge. And the FBI would love to talk to her, too, he imagined.

"What a fine mess," he whispered to the night. "You've managed to not only get her all tangled up in your problems, but now you've gone and gotten your own heart tangled up in . . . in her."

He couldn't leave her now. But he shouldn't, wouldn't kiss her again. He'd keep things all business, he'd put a distance between them, to protect her. He wouldn't lead her on anymore.

Because nothing good could come of this. Gavin didn't have anything to offer a woman like Lacey York. Not anything at all.

As he stared out into the gardens of Bayou le Jardin, wishing he could find the peace Lacey assured him was there, he realized the sad part about all of this. Lacey had everything in the world to offer him, everything a man could ever want.

But Gavin couldn't accept what she was offering.

Lacey lay awake, her eyes centered on

the elaborate canopy of the 150-year-old tester bed that had belonged to her great-great-grandmother. She couldn't sleep, and she didn't want to count sheep.

She wanted to remember the way Gavin had held her and kissed her there on the back gallery. She wanted to remember the way the stars had twinkled, the way the moon had beamed a direct light right down on them, the way the wind had caressed her warm skin, the way Gavin had made her feel like a delicate flower blossoming awake after a long cold winter.

She wanted to remember, and yet she knew she shouldn't. She should just put tonight's revelations and awakenings out of her mind. The memories brought her such pleasure, and such tremendous guilt. She tried to replace the recent memories with other memories, memories of her time spent with Neil, memories of the love they had shared.

Things were becoming blurred in her tired, confused mind. Lacey felt as if a great sheer curtain was covering her, and she wanted to fight to get free of it.

She turned over to stare out the alcove doors onto the small balcony just off her room. She'd left the doors open to the night, but now the temperature had dropped. Tossing on a light robe, she got up to shut out the cold, her white cotton nightgown rippling around her legs as she looked down onto the slumbering garden.

Then she saw him.

Gavin was walking out in the garden. He was shirtless, his jeans hanging low on his hips, the white patch of his bandaged shoulder gleaming starkly against his dark skin. The moonlight touched on him, danced around him, making him look like a statue as he stopped on the path to lean up against the trunk of a towering oak.

He has so much to offer, Lacey thought, her heart going out to the man down in the gardens. She knew this. She had always been a good judge of character. And Gavin Prescott possessed a certain character that was unmistakable in its essence. Aunt Hilda would say he had high moral fiber.

But what would Aunt Hilda say if she knew Lacey was harboring a man on the run, a man in trouble with the law and two very powerful influences?

"She would tell me to follow my heart," Lacey whispered. "She would tell me to watch and pray."

So that's what Lacey did. She prayed for

the lonely figure standing down in her garden. She prayed for the dark knight who'd asked her to rescue him. She'd seen things happen here in this garden. She'd witnessed people bruised and hurting become healed and whole again.

God was in this garden. And God was watching over Gavin Prescott on this beautiful autumn night. Maybe even, God's presence had drawn Gavin out into the trees and flowers, to pray for himself.

Lacey stood there on her balcony, her eyes never leaving the man down below as she asked the Lord to watch over him and protect him from harm. And when Gavin looked up, as if he knew she'd been there all along, Lacey didn't flinch or try to hide away. She looked down at Gavin, and accepted the turmoil that raged inside her heart.

"God will see us through, Gavin," she promised on a low whisper.

She would accept whatever happened. She would support Gavin through this bad time, because he needed her. But she had to keep him at a distance until she could figure out all the emotions she'd tried to deny.

Right now, that help and support was all she could offer him. It might not be nearly enough, but it would have to do for a beginning. Lacey, however, intended to see things through to the end. That was another lesson Aunt Hilda had taught her.

Always finish what you start.

Chapter Seven

"I need to order a few things over the Internet," Gavin told Lacey the next morning. "I should use cash, but I need them quickly. And I'm sure they are monitoring my personal credit cards for any action."

"We have a business credit card," Lacey said. "If you use that, no one could ever trace it back to you."

"You are way too trusting," Gavin replied. "How do you know I won't run up a bill that I can't possibly pay?"

"Is that what you plan on doing?"

They were back in the den just off the kitchen. They'd had a quick breakfast of toast and fruit. And neither of them had mentioned the kisses they'd shared last night or how they'd stared at each other in the moonlight.

But Gavin certainly remembered everything about last night, especially looking up to find Lacey there on the balcony above like a princess from some long-ago romantic tale. Except that he was no prince.

He remembered last night, all right. Remembered, but refused to let things go any further. Maybe that was why he was cranky this morning. Maybe that was why he wanted to question Lacey's seemingly unshakable faith in him. If he could show her that he couldn't be trusted, maybe it would be easier to let her go, to watch her go.

"My plan is to order a cell phone first. It's a new type of phone, just off the market. I can access the Web with it from anywhere in the world. And I can access confidential records, too, with the right codes."

"So you need one of these phones? But why? Can't you access records from this computer?"

He pushed a hand through his spiky hair, then took a long sip of the strong smooth coffee Lacey kept readily available. "Yes, but it's tricky. I have to go in through the back door, so to speak. I can spy on them without being detected, if I'm careful, but I don't want anything to be traced back to you."

"It's a little late to worry about that," she said. "Just do what you need to do, Gavin. We'll figure out the rest."

Gavin heard the frustration in her words. "Regrets, *cara?*"

She wouldn't look at him. Instead, she busied herself with tidying up the already clean room. "I don't regret helping you. I'm just worried."

But she probably regretted kissing him. Gavin knew this in his heart. And how could he blame her? What could he give a woman like Lacey Dorsette York? A woman who came from old money and a strong, noble lineage. Would a woman such as that want to be involved with a man who'd been adopted as a child by a man with new, tainted money? A man, a son, who had resented that adopted father, even while he wanted so very much to please him?

It didn't matter that Gavin's real father had been an honest man of impeccable integrity, or that Gavin's own heritage dated back to Spanish nobility. What mattered now was that he was the son of Senator Edward Prescott, and he was being set up for crimes he didn't commit — framed by his own father. In his mind, Gavin was as tainted and guilty as the senator, simply from guilt by association. And to the world, that was the only kind of guilt that mattered. He'd be branded and ruined before he ever got his day in court. He didn't want Lacey to have to deal with that.

116

"You should be worried," he said after watching her move about the room, her floral sundress falling in graceful folds over her slender legs. Each time she leaned down to pick up a magazine or straighten a pillow, her pearls fell away from her neck in an elegant sweep. Those pearls held a luster, a creamy sheen that came only from being worn so closely to warm skin.

For Gavin, that sheen represented everything good and pure about Lacey. And acted as a constant reminder that he shouldn't touch her, shouldn't want to kiss her again.

Shouldn't want her, period.

But he did, so he resorted to grouchiness in order to hide that want. "Did you hear me?"

Lacey dropped the stack of magazines she'd been organizing onto the long, low coffee table. "I heard you. I need some answers, Gavin."

"I told you why I need the phone."

"Order the phone, order whatever you need. Just tell me the truth. I can handle it."

Gavin reached up a hand to stop yet another reorganization of the neat stack of magazines. "The truth? You want the truth?"

"I think that's fair, considering."

He dropped his hand away, then stared up at her. "Considering that you might be aiding and abetting a criminal, and harboring that very criminal under your roof?"

Lacey sank onto the divan, her blue eyes glimmering like a morning sky full of hope and clarity. "I don't believe you're a criminal. A criminal could have done any number of offending things by now, but you're so intent on finding out the truth — I just know you're innocent."

"Even though the latest news reports have my own father hinting that I'm involved in some sort of cover-up?"

They'd heard that revelation on the early-morning news. The senator, silver haired and impeccably dressed, had given an interview on the steps of his impressive but gaudy New Orleans mansion. "I'm worried about my son," the senator had said with just the right amount of affliction in his deep Southern drawl. "His mother and I have lost sleep, we can't eat. We just want Gavin to know that whatever kind of trouble he's in, we are here to help him. This whole investigation has been a strain on us. I maintain that I am innocent of all charges, but I am deeply distressed that our son might be at the center of all of this. I trusted him with many of my business affairs, but I never dreamed he might be doing anything illegal. I know the truth will come out if this goes to trial. And I hope by then that Gavin will turn himself in and let us help in his defense."

Gavin had been both angered and sickened by his father's smooth but deliberate spiel. If he didn't put all the pieces together, and soon, he'd be the one going off to prison. Put there by his own so-called father. And his loving mother.

Lacey's face remained cool and serene as she looked at him now. "Your father is a smooth operator, no doubt. And I know you're mad and upset by what he said, and by seeing your mother right there with him."

"Ah, my mother," Gavin said. "Didn't she look noble and elegant in her designer suit and flashing diamond solitaire ring? She was the perfect picture of the long-suffering mother and wife."

"Maybe she's putting on a front, to protect you."

Gavin scowled at that. "Nita is only out to protect one person — herself. I saw that today, watching her on that screen. I saw the fear in her eyes. She's not worried about me. She's worried about losing her place in society and that hidden fortune the FBI and the district attorney are trying to locate. The money, honey. That's the key to all of this. And from what my friend Harry Crane is telling me, the money is hidden somewhere not even computer files can trace it."

"You spoke to him on the phone earlier, right?"

"Yes." Gavin nodded. "He seems to be on my side, at least. And he's willing to risk his neck to help me. That counts for something in my book. Now, maybe with Harry's expertise and what I know, I can finally crack the real files — the ones that will lead me to the money and all the records."

Lacey put a hand on his arm this time. The physical contact brought a deep, frustrated longing back into Gavin's soul. He looked down at her hand with such intensity, Lacey pulled it away as if he'd branded her. "Tell me what else you hope to accomplish by cracking into these files."

Gavin let out a breath, wondering how she could read him so well. "Maybe I should start from the beginning."

"That might be best."

She looked so calm, so sure that she almost scared Gavin into stalling again. But Lacey's steadfast belief in him made him want to tell her everything. She deserved that much, at least.

"Okay. You know about the charges being brought against my father?"

She nodded. "Last I heard, he could be indicted for at least seven different counts — everything from bribery and embezzlement to fraud and falsification of records."

"That's right. The FBI wired his offices and our homes — both here in New Orleans and the apartment he keeps in Baton Rouge, and even his vacation home on the Gulf. They think they have a pretty good case against him. But my father is slick. He knows which words to use and which words to avoid whenever he's making a deal. And I know he made all kinds of deals to get the Casa de Oro Casino built in New Orleans. Plus, this was a very big deal for the Currito family, too. They have been trying to go legitimate for years. This casino gave them the perfect opportunity, and so far, from what I'm seeing and what Harry's been able to dig up — they are clean. I think the senator strong-armed them in this case."

He stopped, took another swig of coffee. "I was involved in some of his legitimate deals — just there to make sure the paper flowed correctly — but I was never really a part of the inner circle. I now believe he had others working on some very different deals, with the real paperwork, the real contracts. I was given the accurate, legal versions of certain transactions, probably just to keep me busy. Someone else knows the real scoop. And that someone controls all the clues and secrets to his hidden earnings."

"When did you get suspicious?"

He sat silent for a minute, then said, "Looking back, I remember being uneasy about this long before any contracts were drawn up. But I couldn't put a finger on it. I just assumed because we were dealing with the Curritos that maybe I was being paranoid. But we had meeting after meeting and Sancho Currito himself assured us he wanted to run a clean operation. So the senator promised to back him in the legislature and with the licensing board. He gave the project his complete support, told Sancho he could make things happen. And things did happen. But then when the dust settled, and the casino had only been open a few months — other things started happening, too.

"After the story broke about his possible

arrest and indictment, he called me for a conference. We met at the Audubon Zoo, of all places. He said he had to be careful, because of the wiretapping. He told me he trusted me, and that I had to help him prove his innocence. Like a fool, I believed him. I soaked up the attention. He'd never really needed me before. Now, of course, I can see exactly why he needed me."

He saw the shock and the sympathy surfacing in Lacey's eyes. "You think he set you up?"

"I know he did. He put me on the case. Gave me access to files — documents that would prove he'd done nothing wrong. I thought I was making headway. Between my grunt work and the three other savvy, high-priced lawyers he'd hired, I thought we could actually clear his name. After all, all the government had was the wiretapping tapes and . . . it was doubtful they could prove anything said there. Without witnesses to corroborate what had taken place or explain what the conversations really meant, and without a viable paper trail or any illegal funds turning up, the whole investigation was pretty weak."

Lacey nodded. "So what went wrong? Why did that man try to . . . kill you?"

Gavin touched on his cross, his whole

body going rigid with the memory. "I was too good at my job. I kept digging, wanting desperately to prove that he'd done nothing wrong. After following the supposed money trail that the FBI said would seal the case, I came across some records that didn't quite add up. I found some cash that didn't correspond with all the bank statements and accountant records to which he'd given me access. The cash did correspond with the FBI's investigation, though. Almost down to the penny — except we weren't dealing in pennies. I'm talking millions and millions of dollars.

"So I confronted him, and saw the truth in his eyes that night. Then he turned nasty and defensive, told me I was weak, that I'd never be able to gain any power or prestige if I didn't know how to play the game. He claimed he was doing this for my mother and me — to secure our future. And I told him I didn't need that kind of security."

Gavin paused, leaned back in his chair, his hands held together in front of him as if he were in prayer. He couldn't tell Lacey what he hadn't been able to tell his father, either. That the only security he really wanted was the love of a father, the kind of security every son craves.

"We argued back and forth — him trying to justify all of it and me trying to find some sense of justice in the whole thing. Then he fired me, disowned me, told me to get out. And I reminded him that I didn't owe him anything. I was only required to keep confidential the legitimate transactions I'd been involved in. I wanted to make him sweat, so I threatened him, told him that since I'd just been given my walking papers, I could turn on him. I didn't want to keep the truth away from the authorities. They needed to know what I'd found. That was pretty stupid, but then I wasn't thinking very clearly. I was angry and sick to my stomach.

"After we argued, I found my mother and tried to talk to her, but she was in her element — entertaining and the center of attention. She told me I was overreacting, imagining things. So I decided to leave, but before I left I went into the senator's office and did a little more research on the computer. I found some files, buried deep inside the hard drive — files that the senator probably thought he'd deleted for good. I memorized the codes and wrote down some information, then I headed toward the kitchen. That's when I had the unfortunate luck to run into our friend Randall at the back entrance to the house. He had a gun and he was pointing it at my head."

Lacey lifted her head and closed her eyes. "I don't even want to think about that."

"Believe me, I don't like thinking about it, either. I knew then that I was onto the truth. Randall invited me back inside. Said the senator and Mr. Currito needed to have a word with me. I pretended to agree, then turned to face him. He pushed me forward and I resisted — in a big way. I wasn't about to go under house arrest again. I managed to knock the gun out of his hand and . . . well, you know the rest of the story."

Lacey nodded again. "He pulled the letter opener on you and tried to stab you. Your cross deflected the weapon and saved you."

Gavin leaned forward then to take her hands in his. "Yes. I managed a jab or two at the big man — just long enough to knock him back so I could get away. I left on foot — it's easier to hide that way and I wasn't so sure I could drive anyway. Then after hiding in and out of side streets and alleys most of the night, I wound up in the cathedral."

She wrapped her hands over his. "And

126

that's where I came in, I believe."

Wishing all over again that he'd never seen her sitting there in the morning light, Gavin nodded. "Lacey, that's it. That's all I know, other than they've set up some incriminating records to make me take the fall. I have part of the information I need to get to the real records, but it's not nearly enough. I think I know how to access those records, but they've probably moved them or destroyed them by now."

"That makes sense," she said. "But you think there's more?"

Gavin hung his head, the bone-weary worry making him want to close his eyes and sleep for a week. "I know my father. And I now know how he operates. He is very thorough, very meticulous when it comes to keeping records. He's got it all hidden somewhere — all the transactions, all the deals and all the money. You see, from what I've gathered so far, he uses these secret records as insurance over the people he bullies and bribes. Anyone who has ever needed a political favor from him has been forced to contribute to his campaigns over the years. And he's got records of all of it — what favors were given and how much he needs to extract as payback. And he always expects payback. It took me so long to finally admit that, to finally see what had been there all along."

Lacey got up, her arms going around her midsection as she paced the floor. "That's amazing. All that energy and intelligence wasted. And for what? Power? More money? Greed?"

"All of the above," Gavin said. He got up, too, to still her, to hold his hands on her arms. "It's going to get pretty ugly before it ends, Lacey. Which is why I didn't want to tell you everything."

"But all I know is what you believe to be true. I don't know what you found or . . ." She stopped, stared up at him. "Where did you hide this evidence that you found?"

Gavin dropped his hands and backed away. "Oh, no. You won't get that out of me. That little bit of information would put you in even more danger. I know where it is, but I'm the only one. If they get to me, then it's over. He'll go free."

Lacey stalked across the space between them to grab Gavin by his shirt. "You have to tell me. If something happens to you, then I can alert the authorities. I can make sure he doesn't get away with this."

It was too much for Gavin. He pushed her away. "No. I won't put you at risk like that. They'd . . . I don't want to think about what they'd do to you. Remember, the FBI and the Currito family are probably both hot on our trail, too. They'd all fight dirty, and they'd break you, Lacey. I have to protect you, and I have to keep digging."

"Then I'm going to keep digging with you."

He shook his head. "I told you I only needed a place to hide for a while, and access to a computer. Once I order all the equipment I need, I'm going back to New Orleans."

"And I'm going with you."

Gavin looked down at the woman holding his shirt and realized he had more problems than he'd ever thought possible. The determined look in Lacey's eyes told him that he had two fights on his hands. One with the law and his father and the other with the woman in front of him.

He wasn't sure he was up to either.

Chapter Eight

"Lacey, are you all right? You sound . . . odd."

Lacey bit her lower lip, then tried to find a perky voice before answering her sister's question over the phone. It was just like Lorna to sense something wasn't right, even from hundreds of miles away. "I'm fine. Couldn't be better, actually. I was just in the middle of making a salad to have later for lunch, and then I have to do a rather tedious inventory of some of the things I ordered in New Orleans." *Oh, and by the way, I have a very handsome and mysterious man here with me, and we're hiding out from the FBI, his father and the Spanish Mafia. And I've only known him about three days.*

Lorna's doubtful sigh caused Lacey to stop talking to herself. "Oh, okay. I was just surprised to find you home so soon."

"Yes, I cut my trip short. Lots to do here, though."

"Well, I called to leave a message, but since I got you instead of the machine, I'll tell you — we'll be home by this weekend.

Think you can handle things for a few more days?"

If you only knew.

"Yes," Lacey replied. "All is quiet here. It rained for two days — would you believe a hurricane is forming in the Gulf — so the construction work has been postponed, and Justin is still gone. I told the part-time landscapers to take a couple of days off, too. It's too soggy for anyone to work and the weather is so unpredictable. I haven't heard a peep from the Babineaux clan and I haven't had a chance to ride into the village to see how Josh and Kathryn are doing with all the official business of Jardin."

"I'm sure they're running things just fine without Aunt Hilda there," Lorna replied. "Have you heard from her?"

"Ah, no," Lacey said, turning as Gavin walked into the kitchen. She pressed a finger to her lips to remind him to stay quiet. He went on full alert, but she smiled to reassure him. "Lorna, listen, everything is okay here. You just have fun with Mick and get some rest. You're going into the second trimester of your pregnancy, remember?"

"I remember every waking hour," Lorna said. "And . . . I guess that's why I just

131

wanted to hear your voice. I was thinking about you this morning."

Lacey knew why her sister had been thinking of her. She'd lost her baby at five months. Lorna was approaching five months in her own pregnancy. "It won't happen to you, Lorna," Lacey said, more to reassure herself than her sister. "You're going to have a healthy, beautiful baby."

"From your lips to God's ears," Lorna said. "I get so scared, and so emotional. Must be the hormones."

"That's it," Lacey replied, ignoring the tears misting her own eyes. "Mick will take care of you, both of you. And you have wonderful doctors in both Louisiana and Mississippi."

"I know, I know. I think I'm just worrying about nothing . . . and everything. Lacey, what if Mick isn't ready for all of this?"

Concerned for her sister, Lacey frowned. "What do you mean? Are you two having problems?"

"No," Lorna said, laughing shakily. "It's just . . . well, Mick has been so sweet and patient. You know, he was so understanding about my achluphobia, but in spite of my unreasonable fear of the dark, we're very much in love. We've only been

132

married a few months, and I've just now learned to overcome my fear. My being cured is tentative at best, even though the therapist tells me I'm doing fine. I don't have anything to obsess about, I suppose. So now I'm obsessing about whether Mick really wants a child or not."

"Has Mick said that — that he wasn't ready for children?"

"No. He seems to be on cloud nine. He's just as happy as I am — that is, when I'm not worrying."

"So what's the problem?"

She heard her sister's long sigh. "Well, we're just such an . . . overwhelming family. I hope it's not all too much, too soon, for Mick."

Lacey couldn't help but smile. "Lorna, Mick is so in love with you, I don't think he can be any more overwhelmed. He's pretty much past that point. And from what I've seen, he can't wait to be a father. I think you're worrying yourself about nothing. But I certainly understand. It's only natural, honey, to have these feelings. Your life has changed so much in the past few months. And even good, positive changes can be frightening sometimes."

"Are you sure you're all right?" Lorna asked. "You sound almost too chirpy, too philosophical. Lucas is the poet, not you. You're too practical. Why are you acting so strange?"

"I'm trying to cheer *you* up, remember?" Lacey replied, wondering how she was going to convince her sister that she was okay. "I'm trying to show you that change is good."

Gavin watched her with each word, making it hard to focus on what she was saying to her sister.

"Things are changing," Lorna replied. "I just thought maybe . . . maybe we shouldn't have left you all alone. I mean, we've never left each other alone, ever. Someone has always been there. And now, Lacey, well —"

"Stop it," Lacey said, frustration causing her to snap. "Lorna, I don't want you or Lucas feeling sorry for me. I told you I'm fine, just fine."

"Now you *really* don't sound fine," Lorna said. "What's going on there?"

Lacey sighed, pushed a hand through her hair. "Just some of those changes we're discussing, I suppose. I'm learning to enjoy the solitude here."

She looked over at Gavin and thought about how her own life had changed in just a matter of days. But then, that was the thing about life. You never knew from one day to the next, good or bad. "Are you going to be all right?" she asked her sister.

"Yes, I feel better now," Lorna replied. "I just needed someone . . . I just needed family. Mick's folks are great, but I sure miss Bayou le Jardin and all of you."

"It's different here, too," Lacey said sincerely. "It's odd not having everyone around, but as I said I needed this time for some changes of my own." Deciding to change the subject, she added, "But I'm sure Lucas and Willa aren't missing any of us. I haven't heard from them, either."

"They're too involved with each other to think about calling home," Lorna replied. Then she picked right back up on Lacey's life. "Hope you're not lonely. Our next mission is to find someone for you. We want you to be happy again, too. I can start pondering how to make that happen, just to take my mind off the fears of parenthood."

Lacey glanced over at Gavin. The intensity of his gaze made her want to stumble and stutter, but she knew Lorna would pick up on that. So in what she hoped was a calm voice, she said, "No need to ponder about me, sister. I'm . . . okay, really. I was a little blue in New Orleans, but I'm holding my own, so don't worry about any matchmaking on my part."

Gavin raised a dark eyebrow in what looked like a challenge to that statement, but the impact of his eyes stayed the same, steady and sure and very direct. To avoid that directness, Lacey turned her back to him. "And besides, you'll be home soon. All of you. In the meantime, I'll track down Aunt Hilda to tell her you're all right and you're having a blast." *And I will not tell her that there is a new man in my life — too many extenuating circumstances.*

She wished she could tell Lorna. But she couldn't. Not yet. Lacey had never been one to keep secrets, but this time she didn't have any choice. Her entire family would be up in arms about this particular situation. She'd explain everything when the time was right. Or maybe Gavin would be gone out of her life and she'd never have to explain her actions at all.

Lorna's voice echoed through the phone line again, jarring Lacey out of her secretive musings. "I'd appreciate that. Give Aunt Hilda our love if you talk to her. Well, guess I'll see you at the end of the week."

Lacey hung up to find Gavin's gaze still on her. "Is your sister all right?"

136

"Yes. She was just checking in. We're all very close and . . . it's been a while since we've each gone our separate ways like this. We're still adjusting to it, I suppose."

"Obviously." His grin held a devastating dazzle. "Matchmaking, huh? I wonder how your sister would feel about me?"

"She'd probably take one look at you and tell me you're not nearly good enough for me."

"And she'd be right," he countered, dead serious.

"I was joking. My siblings are nosy and bossy, but they know when to draw the line."

He leaned over the counter. "Well, I'm sure they'd draw the line on me, in a heartbeat."

"They don't know you. Maybe one day they will."

"I doubt that." He got a faraway look in his eyes that made Lacey miss him already. A look that only reminded her that she didn't know him, either.

To hide her confusing feelings, she started talking about Lorna. "Lorna is having a bad case of the jitters, what with being married and with child — so many changes, but good ones."

"Are you worried about her baby?"

Lacey covered the salad and put it in the refrigerator. Since she couldn't bring herself to tell him about her own miscarriage, she only nodded. "Natural, I think, to worry about a child coming into the world. Lorna was feeling kind of insecure, a bit emotional. She just needed some reassurance."

He came close, his hands resting on the corners of the wide butcher-block table. "I just wondered. You looked so sad when you were discussing it."

"Did I?" She shrugged, picked up the bottle of salad dressing she'd just mixed. To hide her nervousness, she shook the sealed glass carafe with all her might to make sure the fresh-minced garlic would mix with the olive oil and vinegar. "Probably because I've always wanted children of my own. Having a new niece or nephew will be the next best thing."

He stood there, still in borrowed clothes — courtesy of Lucas's closet this time — still dark and brooding and mysterious. "Did you and your husband —"

"Did we want children?" She whirled to put the dressing in beside the salad. "Of course." She glanced over the contents of the refrigerator, making sure she'd done everything to prepare for lunch. She had, and now she'd run out of things to do and it was just nine o'clock in the morning, and Gavin wanted to know why she didn't have a child. "It . . . didn't happen for us."

She could feel him there, silent and still. It felt as if he knew her pain. It felt as if he knew exactly what was going through her mind. Impossible, of course. And yet, she didn't dare look at him. Maybe she should whip up some blueberry muffins, too. Although she wasn't the cook in the family, it would keep her busy.

"Well," he said at last, "I just came in to tell you those deliveries should arrive tomorrow. A new cell phone with a completely new number and better security measures, a laptop, so I can check e-mails with an anonymous password and remailer, and some other things I'll need in order to crack and secure all the files."

"I see." She finally managed to look up at him, and she hoped that her face was serene and blank. "So what do we do until then?"

"We wait and watch," Gavin told her.

"Or as my aunt would say, we watch and pray."

"We could do a little of both."

"That means we have the whole day ahead of us."

He lifted his brows in another challenge. "*Sì*. But the sky is dark and the wind is chilly. Any ideas?"

Lots of ideas. But not the kind that kept things professional and detached. And not the kind that involved watching and praying. Although she sure needed to do both.

"I have some work to do in the shop. You could come along, if you'd like. You can play on the laptop there while I tag and inventory."

"Or I could play tag with you."

The mischievous look in his espresso-colored eyes only reminded her that she was supposed to keep her distance. And only made her want to spend the day playing tag with him.

Watch and pray, Lacey, she reminded herself. Then because she resented the way he made her want to throw caution to the wind, she said, "I can't concentrate on my work if you insist on flirting, Gavin."

"I can't concentrate period, if you insist I hang around you all day."

She pivoted, fidgeting with the dish towels and the fresh flowers she'd picked for the center of the work island. "Then stay here at the house, or go for a walk in the gardens."

"I did all of my walking last night."

She stopped fidgeting, looked back at him. "So I noticed."

"Did you, now?"

She blushed. He smiled.

"I couldn't sleep," she admitted. "And yes, I saw you walking in the gardens."

"And I saw you up there on your balcony."

"Oh, really, did you, now?" she mimicked, enjoying the way he tipped his head and grinned at her.

"Yes, and I wondered what you were thinking."

She told him the truth, her eyes holding his. "I was thinking that you need my prayers, that you are a good and decent man who's gotten caught up in something dishonorable and indecent."

He lowered his head, looked uncomfortable. "Lacey, you amaze me. You shouldn't be so trusting, so sure."

"Are you telling me that what I feel in my heart is wrong?"

"I'm telling you that I'm not so decent or good. I've been blind, I've been careless and I've made some really bad decisions lately. And looking back, I think I knew all along. I knew he was a criminal and I just looked the other way. That has to be the

141

worst kind of sin."

"He's supposed to be your father, Gavin. If not by blood, then at least in the eyes of the law. Any man would hope that his father is the best, not the worst. There is no sin in that."

"I hoped it," he said, his voice low and husky. "But hoping and praying didn't win out this time."

"Then we have to keep on hoping and praying," she said quietly and with complete conviction.

"What if it's too late?"

"It's never too late when you turn to Christ. I watched you out in the garden last night and I knew He was there with you. It's going to be all right, Gavin."

"Maybe, but for now no more long walks at night," he said. "Instead, maybe we should just take a walk together, in the daylight."

She laughed then. "How about this? I do have some work to do in the shop. There should be several deliveries already waiting on the enclosed side porch for me to unpack and I'm sure more will be delivered today or tomorrow. You could come with me, if you promise to behave. Then we can take the salad and fruit I made for lunch and go on a picnic — if the rain holds off.

I'll show you the Chapel in the Garden. It's in the forest and it's lovely this time of year."

He pushed away from the counter, his gaze moving over her face, stopping on her mouth. "In spite of your endearing attempts to save my rotten soul, I think I like this plan."

Too late to tell him maybe this wasn't such a good idea. If he looked at her that way on the picnic, she wouldn't be able to eat a morsel of food. "Okay. Why don't you grab the paper. You can read it, at least, while I work. Maybe do the crossword puzzle."

"And maybe catch up on the latest political news."

"Just skip the headlines," she said, remembering that the whole Prescott-Currito scandal had been splashed across the front in bold black print.

"No, I think it might be smart to go back over that article with a fine-tooth comb," Gavin said as he took the paper and folded it underneath his arm. "Maybe I'll hit on something, remember something, see something that can help."

"Very smart." She glanced around the tidy kitchen. "Well, lunch is all set. I'll just pack the salad and other things in a cooler

143

and we can get on with our day." Although how she was supposed to put in a normal day's work with him about, she didn't know.

"I'll help."

Together they loaded in cups, plates and the food and drink, their fingers brushing now and then in the effort. Gavin tossed her the paper and lifted the cooler by the handle. "Lacey?"

"Hmm?" She was walking ahead of him, her mind already on the work waiting for her. Her mind trying very hard to resist the way he called her name in that exotic accent, and the way his warm fingers felt against her skin.

"Thank you."

She turned to find him standing there staring at her, his eyes a deep, rich dark chocolate that glistened in the gray morning light. "For what?" she asked on a breathless whisper.

"For everything. For not asking the wrong questions, or the right ones, either, for that matter. For reminding me about my faith. For . . . believing in me."

Her gaze moved from his face to the cross medallion. "I do believe in you, Gavin. I realize I don't know everything about you, and I don't know or even begin to understand why I trust you. But I don't think I'll regret helping you. You won't let me down."

"I hope not," he said. Then he hefted the cooler and started walking. "I sure hope not."

The Antique Garden was a quaint little building that had once been the overseer's house, Lacey explained. In recent years it had been the groundskeeper's cottage. But a few years ago, Justin Hayes had bought a bigger house in the village.

"That's when I got the idea to turn this place into an antique and gift shop," Lacey said.

"It suits you," Gavin said as he strolled through the elegant clutter. Nothing tacky or gaudy here. The place was just like its owner, pure class. It was a mixture of old and new, a mixture of scented candles and fresh flowers, a mixture of feminine appeal and timeless designs.

Lacey looked around, pride evident in her eyes. "Well, I don't turn a huge profit . . . but I needed something to do after . . . after Neil died." She touched a hand to a brocade tapestry. "Sometimes I think Justin moved out of here just to give me the space. I had dabbled in antiques for years as the unofficial buyer for the house. When Neil and I were stationed in Europe, I shopped for things and shipped them home. After Neil died and I came back here, Justin was very sweet. He encouraged me to expand, spread my wings. Then the whole family got behind him and gently urged me to go for it. I have to admit, the work kept me from going crazy, kept me centered. It still does."

"And this Justin — you and he are close?" Gavin couldn't help the ugly streak of jealousy in his words. And he sure wasn't ready to justify it.

Looking baffled, Lacey finally smiled. "He's a good friend. We've known him since grade school and he's . . . well, he's just Justin. He's always been around. He's worked here at Bayou le Jardin for most of his life, in one capacity or another. He loves the land and the gardens. Very protective of this place."

"And you? Is Justin protective of you?"

She lowered her head, glanced away out into the gardens. "Sometimes, yes. But he understands how things are."

Gavin hoped so. He hoped this Justin Hayes knew exactly how things were. But then, Gavin didn't have any claims over Lacey. None at all. And he'd be gone soon.

Gone. While the gallant Justin would always be around.

Lacey turned on the radio, bringing a soft, classical instrumental tune out over the still air.

"Ah, I know this music," Gavin said. "My mother always played classical music in the house, and she insisted I attend the symphony with the senator and her. Even though, growing up, I preferred rock and blues."

"Which you played loudly in your room while under house arrest, I bet."

"Exactly. Just another part of the rebel in me. However, I do have an avid appreciation of the finer things in life, such as your music."

"It is very soothing," Lacey said. "It helps me when I'm here alone. I don't particularly like the quiet."

Gavin pondered that statement while he picked up a delicate china cup done in a pattern of yellow roses. "I can certainly understand that. You've been through a lot, so much tragedy. And yet, you've found beauty in the ruins."

She lowered her head, dropped her tote bag on a chair. "I've never looked at it that way. But there is always beauty to be found — or at least that's what Aunt Hilda would say. She'd like you, I'm sure."

"Maybe one day —"

"Yes, one day," Lacey said. Then she turned to click on lamps and switch on the small laptop computer sitting on a walnut desk. "I'll make a fresh pot of coffee. There's a small kitchen and half bath in the back."

Gavin watched as she hurried away, her long sweeping denim skirt flying out behind her, her ruffly, heavy white cotton long-sleeved blouse looking like a trail of clouds around her shoulders. The scent of her perfume wafted through the air with a hint of magnolia and gardenia, every bit as feminine and dainty as the things with which she surrounded herself.

You won't let me down.

Those words seemed to echo throughout the still shop with the overtures and crescendos of the music. She'd said them as a statement, as if he were her one last hope. Lacey had had so many letdowns, so much pain in her life, and yet she still looked for the beauty, she still managed to find the simple pleasures in life here with her treasures, here amidst the flowers and trees of this ancient garden. She was like a sleeping princess waiting to be awakened. Holding out for a hero?

Gavin couldn't be that hero. He couldn't be the one to awaken her. He wanted to — oh, how he wanted to be the one. But he was afraid Lacey had pinned too many hopes on him. He was sure that in the end, he would have to let her down.

Because right now he didn't see any way out of this situation. Things didn't look good. People would question his motives, his loyalty to his father. They'd wonder how he could have worked so closely with Prescott for so long, without even knowing what the man had been doing.

And Gavin had to wonder that very thing himself. How had he let himself be duped so blatantly? He thought back over the years, thought back about how he'd worked as an intern in the senator's offices from high school all the way through college. How he'd clerked and sweated, running errands, carrying important documents here and there, doing whatever was needed, all the way through law school. How convenient for the senator that Gavin had decided to stay in the city and attend Tulane — at his mother's insistence, of course. How very clear now as the memories came flooding back.

The memories. It had always been his mother. Nita had always been the buffer between Edward and Gavin, had always been the one to coach him, guide him, in matters concerning his father. His mother had been the one to push Gavin into working for his father, had been there to oversee each move, each decision regarding her son. When he really thought about it, the senator had always kept him at a distance, at arm's length. He'd always been just outside the powerful circle of employees and friends the senator kept near. But his mother had always been right there, coaching, encouraging, making him be a part of things he really didn't want to be involved in at all. And now Gavin could see why, could see that he'd been manipulated so prettily and so neatly, it was almost a crime.

Almost a crime.

He grabbed the newspaper, his heart pumping with adrenaline and dread. *"Está en todo."*

Lacey came back into the room then. "Did you say something, Gavin?"

Gavin couldn't speak. He stood there staring at her, his mind reeling with a horrible, cold suspicion.

"Gavin, what is it?"

"She's been involved all along," he finally said in English. "I was just too blind, too stupid to see what was right in front of my eyes."

"What are you talking about?" Lacey asked as she came over to scan the paper he had clutched in his hands.

"Look," he said, pointing to the picture of his parents. "Tell me, what do you see?"

Lacey gave him a worried look, then took the paper from him, scanning the picture and the caption. "I see your parents. They're smiling, holding hands. It's a normal picture, in spite of all their troubles."

Gavin grabbed the paper from her, then tossed it down on the counter, anger bubbling over inside him. "*Sí*, it looks perfectly normal, doesn't it? My mother looks like every other society matron in New Orleans. A model citizen, involved in charity work, social functions, a renowned entertainer, a renowned hostess. A woman who is clearly standing by the man she loves."

"Yes," Lacey said. Then she placed a hand on his arm. "I know how that must upset you, Gavin. Maybe you should try calling your mother again. I'm sure in spite of how this looks, she's probably very concerned about you. I mean, you're her son. She'd have to be worried."

He pushed away, pivoted, his hands

rushing through his hair. "You'd think that, wouldn't you? It's all just so normal, so carefully staged, so calculated."

"I'm afraid I'm not quite following you," Lacey said.

He let out a frustrated sigh, then shook his head. "Lacey, it's right there — it's been right there all along. My mother — she has to be the one."

"The one? Gavin, please tell me what this is all about."

He paced the confines of the shop, his eyes not seeing the antique jewelry lining the counter or the curio cabinet full of delicate china vases. "It all makes sense now. This is the missing piece, the part of the puzzle I couldn't quite put together."

"Which is?"

"My mother," he said on a disgusted breath. "You see, I figured out that someone had been carrying the documents, the records for all these illegal deals. Someone very close to my father, someone who had protected him even while that someone was duping me. I've racked my brains, going over all the names and files of his associates. But I kept coming up empty. But now, now I have the sick feeling that I know who the front man has been all along."

Lacey's face showed understanding at last. "Except it's not a man at all, right?"

Gavin's gaze held hers. "No, not a man. But a woman. A very clever, very conniving woman."

"Your mother?" Lacey asked, astonished.

"My mother," Gavin answered, equally astonished. "My very own mother may have betrayed me, Lacey. How am I supposed to fight that? How do I prove my innocence when my own mother has been working against me all along?"

Chapter Nine

"You can't be serious? How can you be sure?"

Gavin looked down at the paper again, wishing he wasn't serious. "I'm not sure. But this is the key, Lacey. This is why I have to go back. I have to get to my mother's records, find out where she's been hiding all the transactions, and all of the money. Up until now, I've been concentrating on the senator's files. I need to get to my mother's personal accounts, too."

Lacey slumped down in the high-back chair behind the desk. "So you think your mother is the go-between from your father to whoever he's accepted bribes from?"

"It makes sense now," Gavin said. "I've thought about this. Last night, when I walked through the gardens, I went over my life, in slow motion, trying to see where I'd gone wrong, trying to accept that maybe I'd inadvertently done something illegal or dishonest. And it didn't make much sense. I worked hard, in spite of how badly my adopted father treated me." He stopped, hit his hand on the paper. "That man . . . did things to me that should have made me run for my life."

"What kind of things?" Lacey asked in a slow, cautious voice, as if she didn't really want to know.

And Gavin didn't want to tell her. Not yet. "Let's just say that he enjoyed inflicting punishment and pain. There was no pleasing him, ever. But the one thing that kept me sane was my mother. She was always right there between us, defending me, begging him to give me another chance. I knew I was loved — my mother loved me, taught me the ways of the church, sent me to private Christian schools where I learned the Golden Rule, and where I felt safe and accepted."

"That's good, at least," Lacey said, her hand reaching out to take his. "You have a solid foundation."

Gavin almost pulled away, but he needed her touch right now. "My mother always seemed so devout, so sure in her faith, or so it seemed. My *abuela*, Madre Selia we called her, she was very religious, very firm in her faith." He touched a hand to the medallion. "She gave me this right before she died a few years ago. It belonged to her mother. I often wondered why she didn't

155

pass it down to my mother instead of me."

"Maybe your grandmother saw your strength and honor and wanted you to have this, Gavin. To remember where that strength and honor comes from."

He looked at her, seeing the goodness and pureness in her beautiful face. "And she didn't see those things in my mother?"

Lacey glanced away, then looked back at him, her gaze sincere and completely honest. "I can't answer that."

"It would seem no one can. Nita has hidden her true colors so very well."

"But you're still not sure."

"No, but it's beginning to sink in. I don't want to accuse my own mother, but it just makes perfect sense. All along, she pushed me toward him. She involved me in everything she could — his business holdings, his law firm. And yet, when I really think about it, I wasn't a part of anything at all. I was just a pawn in their plans. Just a part of the family. And you know what they say about that — *en familia*. It was important that I remained within the family, even if I wasn't welcomed. They had to keep me close, keep me pacified, so I wouldn't find out the truth."

"Because they knew what you would be forced to do," Lacey said, her hand holding tightly to his. "You would have to tell the truth, seek justice. And now you're going to have to do just that."

Gavin didn't answer right away. To put his own parents in jail, to turn on them completely — it didn't set well with him. He felt sick to his stomach. But he reminded himself that Senator Edward Prescott had sent a henchman to stop Gavin. Obviously the senator had no qualms about family loyalty. No, he just demanded a different kind of loyalty, the kind Gavin couldn't give him.

As if sensing his dilemma, Lacey said, "Gavin, you have to do what's right, no matter how much it hurts."

"*Sí*. But not if they can get to me first."

"I hope you're wrong about all of this," she replied, her eyes wide. "I mean, we're talking about your *parents*, Gavin. Surely they wouldn't do something so vile, so underhanded to their own son."

Gavin reminded himself of how very innocent Lacey was. And how very trusting. "Money and power make people do strange things, *cara*."

She gave him a fierce, protective look. "Well, if this is true, they won't get away with it. Just tell me what I can do to help."

Gavin felt something deep inside as he

157

stood there looking at the golden-haired woman sitting beside him. The feeling was raw in its intensity, just comforting. Her eyes held such a sweet innocence that he could almost see heaven shining there. Lacey represented what faith was all about. Her belief in the goodness of life both humbled and amazed Gavin. And made him want to hold her close, just to cleanse some of the darkness from his own soul.

Instantly forgetting that he was supposed to keep his distance, he pulled her hand to his mouth, kissed her fingers. "I really don't want you any more involved in this, Lacey. It was dangerous from the start and now it's even worse. I can't trust any of them. And they must know by now that I have part of the information. I cracked some of the passwords and codes. They just don't know which ones I have and they can't be sure. So they will try to capture me or kill me, and if they can't do that, they'll make it look like I was the inter-loper."

"What are you going to do next?"

He dropped her hand, then pointed to the paper. "My parents always hold an elaborate ball each fall to kick off the holiday season. It's a costume ball, very fancy and very crowded with members of the

Mardi Gras krewe to which they belong. Everyone who's anyone in New Orleans will be there, along with some gate-crashers, too."

"Are you going to be a gate-crasher?"

He nodded. "I think I am. If I can get in when they're too busy entertaining to notice, I can get access to the rest of the data. It will be the best time, because even if they catch me, they wouldn't dare make a fuss. It would ruin the party, you understand? I just hope they haven't moved the data or destroyed it yet."

"How will you get in?"

Gavin smiled then, a wry smile that didn't bring any laughter to his heart. "Why, in costume, of course. I'm going to hide in plain sight, disguised as a normal, everyday, party-going, presumably invited guest."

Lacey got up, put her hands on his shoulders. "Then I'll be there with you. I'll dress in costume, too. I can be your lookout, your watchdog, whatever you call it."

"No." Gavin shook his head, removed her hands from his arms. "You are not going to be a part of this operation, Lacey. Absolutely not."

"Yes, I absolutely am," she replied, bob-

159

bing her head. "Gavin, look around you. I have the perfect setup to create costumes for both of us. I have old dresses, uniforms, disguises. We use them when we dress up for candlelight tours during the Christmas season."

"So we'll march in there as Scarlett and Rhett?"

She smiled, shook her head, made him want to smile in spite of the serious situation. "Too obvious, and we don't want to be obvious."

"We don't want to be conspicuous *or* obvious, Lacey. We need to blend in, stay close to the walls, and keep to the crowd." Then he stepped back. "Listen to me. I'm talking as if I've already agreed to let you go with me."

"I am going," she said, her blue eyes sparkling like a distant shore. "I can help you, Gavin. You can't risk doing this alone."

He ran a hand through his hair. "I suppose it would look less obvious if we were a couple. A lone man walking around might raise eyebrows. They'll be waiting and watching, so security will be tight."

"Exactly," she said, waving a hand. "We have to come up with costumes that are tasteful, yet not too attention grabbing. What's the theme?"

"Theme?" He grabbed the paper again. "The party is mentioned in this article. It says they intend to go on with tradition in spite of their political troubles, so as not to disappoint all their many friends and associates." He grunted in disgust. "That is so very like my parents."

"We'll use that to our advantage," Lacey replied, ever optimistic. "The theme, Gavin?"

He scanned the lengthy article again. "Venetian Ball."

"Perfect. Powder and wigs. I can get my hands on both. And I have costumes. I can alter what I have here and there and come up with something. When is the ball?"

"Friday night. But, Lacey —"

"Hush," she said, grabbing the small cooler by the handle, then shoving it into his hands. "Let's forget work and go for that walk. We have to hash out a plan."

Gavin could only follow her lead — for now. He'd just have to find a way to do this without her. "You know, if I didn't know better, I'd almost think you're having way too much fun with this."

"Not really," she explained as she tugged him out onto the tiny covered side porch, past the stacked boxes she had yet to unpack and inventory. "I am just a woman

161

who likes to stay occupied. I like to plan things out and see them set into motion." She turned to face him, her expression very serious now. "And I like to finish what I start."

Gavin's heart shuddered at that remark. She was very stubborn, and so very beautiful, he had to protect her whether she liked it or not. But he wanted her to understand how things were, too. "Even things that involve espionage and possible murder?"

"That's the challenge," she said, laughing now and shrugging. "I've never done murder and espionage before."

Gavin stopped, then tugged her around, the sick feeling in his gut making him jumpy. "Lacey, this is serious. We're not playing some sort of game here."

Her eyes darkened and she stopped smiling. "I know that, Gavin. I pretty much figured that out the day I saw you coming down that aisle in the cathedral. And I will behave in a very serious manner once we're . . . uh . . . undercover, I can assure you."

"But?"

She lifted an arm, indicating their surroundings. "But right now, the clouds are billowy even if they do look like rain later, and the fall leaves are whirling all around us. We have a plan, which we will discuss at length and finalize to perfection. In the meantime, I want to take your mind off all your troubles. If we go to the garden, I know God will listen, and He will guide us."

She was so innocent, of course. She couldn't know what she was doing to him by offering that one small hope, by offering some time, just time, to forget the world beyond the gates of Bayou le Jardin. It would be so easy to shut the outside world away, to stay hidden in these lush, soothing gardens with her for close to forever. Lacey had apparently been doing that herself, for years. But Gavin knew that for him it was an impossible dream. He just didn't think God would be listening to his silent pleas for guidance.

And yet, he couldn't refuse *her*. Just a few hours of peace, that's all he would accept. Just for the memories. After that, he'd go back to his original intention, which was to slip away. And besides, he really didn't want to delve into just how much his own mother was involved in this scam right now. The thought of that sickened him.

He stared at Lacey as she grabbed a lightweight blue sweater to ward off the autumn chill. She looked so trusting, so . . . pure. He wanted some of that purity for himself, to get the bad taste out of his mouth and the bad feeling out of his insides. "A picnic, *sí?* That . . . would be nice."

She took his hand again, and he watched her as the wind caressed her golden hair and lifted those enticing white ruffles away from her shoulders and throat, only to expose the ever-present glistening strand of perfect pearls.

"Welcome to my garden, Gavin," she said as she tugged hair off her face.

Gavin allowed her to pull him along, and somewhere between the Japanese elm trees and the towering moss-draped cypresses he accepted that he'd finally lost his heart completely and forever.

And because of that, he knew his troubles had just become much, much worse.

The forest was rich with the hues of autumn. They followed a well-worn path that carried them between century-old moss-draped live oaks and craggy-kneed bald cypress trees. Sprinkled in between, tallow trees with leaves upturned in brilliant shades of burgundy and red shot up like sparks from a fire. The woods were ablaze with fall. The very air smelled of ancient, rich earth combined with damp, refreshing wind.

Earth, wind and fire, Gavin thought as he watched Lacey. She moved like a forest creature among the flowers and shrubs. She looked so natural here in her element. And she was natural — in every deed, in every action. From her simply styled hair to her minimal use of makeup to the very essence of her being, Lacey was real, genuine, honest, graceful, unhurried and unabashed.

Belleza. Beautiful.

Gavin had to remind himself to breathe. He'd never been so affected by a woman. He'd had lots of girlfriends, lots of lady friends, lots of women, all of whom would gladly have married him for his father's money and power, if not for love.

Some of them had actually claimed to love him.

But Gavin had always held back. He'd always kept his distance. Somewhere deep inside his soul, he knew that there was such a thing as real love. And he had been waiting to find it, even if he didn't believe he deserved it.

He looked at Lacey in her pearls and ruffles and felt his heart falling away from his body like a leaf gently letting go of a tree. It was as if something dark and decadent had died inside his soul, and in its place something new and clean had emerged to be reborn. And he wondered if Lacey and her fabled Aunt Hilda might be on to something.

Maybe this place did heal people. Maybe these vast, never-ending gardens did bring a perfect peace, a renewed hope, a rebirth to lost souls. Maybe here, in this secluded retreat, he could find the path back home again.

Another impossible dream?

He lowered his head, closed his eyes in a quick, gentle prayer, then glanced up to find Lacey looking back at him. "Gavin?"

"Yes?"

"Are you doing okay back there?"

He shrugged, not yet ready to reveal all that was in his heart. "I'm just a bit over-whelmed. This place is — well, I've never seen anything so beautiful."

Lacey nodded her understanding. "The chapel is right around this curve. There's a grape arbor between the chapel and the family cemetery. We can picnic there, if you want."

He did want. He wanted this kind of peace as a constant in his life. He wanted *her* in his life. He wanted to wake up knowing he had something pure and simple and precious to get him through each day. He wanted to wake up with her next to him, and go to sleep with her by his side each night. He wanted to experience God's rich and unconditional blessings with the woman who had shown him that hope never dies.

But first, he had to finish the job. He had to get rid of the ugliness, the evil in his life. Gavin followed Lacey to the long narrow grape arbor, but before he entered the shelter of the overhanging vines and intricately woven arched trellises, he made a promise to God.

I will come back here one day. To her. And I will turn my life over to You, to thank You each and every day for sending her to me.

"Is this spot all right?" Lacey asked him, pointing to a high-backed wooden bench nestled in the middle of the sun-dappled trellises.

"It's perfect," Gavin replied, glad the dark clouds had parted for a little while.

But he knew it wouldn't be completely perfect, that the dark clouds wouldn't go away until he could come back here and claim her for his own.

Right now he'd just have to settle for this one afternoon with her. He intended to make the most of it.

Chapter Ten

Lacey decided she'd just have to make the best of the situation. Now that they were here, her cheerful mood, which she told herself had been for Gavin's sake anyway, had vanished completely, to be replaced with the old doubts and insecurities. Why on earth had she brought Gavin here, of all places? Here where her husband and her child were buried just a few yards away, here where she'd been married in the tiny chapel, where she'd pledged her heart and soul to another man.

Had she forgotten that pledge in a few short days? Had she become so caught up in the adventure, the enticement of being with Gavin, that she'd forsaken the life she'd had before? But then, she told herself bitterly, that life was over now, had been over for a very long time. And she had been so very lonely. And starved for something, someone to come into her life. She needed to be needed.

And right now, today, Gavin needed some quiet time to reflect on all the horrible things happening in his life. Lacey couldn't imagine being betrayed by family, by your own parents. It didn't make any sense to her at all.

She told herself that Gavin was just as lonely and needy as she was right now.

She shouldn't let *her* loneliness and neediness cloud her better judgment, though. She shouldn't let her need for adventure and . . . something, anything exciting to happen overshadow her need to stay sane and comfortable and safe in her self-imposed seclusion. This might be exciting to her, but Gavin's world was crashing down around him. She needed to remember that, too.

Help me, Lord, she silently prayed.

Wishing she had someone to confide in, Lacey busied herself with spreading out the picnic. She should pray for guidance, pray for these treacherous thoughts and feelings to leave her system. She could confide in the Lord. He knew her every thought.

I need to be logical again, she told herself. I need to go back to the safe, boring Lacey, the lovable Lacey that everyone depended on, everyone counted on.

And what about Gavin? she asked herself. Isn't he counting on you now, too?

She silently asked God to show her the right path.

The dark-skinned hand on her arm made her stop, look up. Gavin was watching her with that intense look again. His accented question only reminded her of how very different this man was from her husband. "Are you in a hurry here for some reason?"

To Lacey, his very words seemed to indicate words the Father might ask her, too. Why was she worrying and hurrying? God would show her the way, whether she liked that way or not.

She dropped the napkins she'd been frantically unfolding. "No . . . I mean, I thought you'd be hungry by now."

"I am," he said, taking her by the arms to pull her down onto the long wooden bench. "But you're buzzing around like a cute little bee. I thought this was going to be our special time to forget the rest of the world."

Lacey glanced toward the cemetery enclosed behind a white wrought-iron picket fence and gate. Ivy clung to the spiked balustrades, its green vines twisting in the wind much the same way she was twisting up inside right now. "It is. I mean, it can be. I'm sorry. I guess my mind just got to racing. We have so much to talk about, a lot of ground to cover before the week's out."

"Stop, then," he said as he placed her hands in her lap. "Just sit there and let me take care of you for a change."

She felt her heart fluttering to a wary standstill. It had been so very long since anyone had offered to do that. Lacey always assumed it was her job to take care of everyone else. It had been that way for such a long time. And now this man who had so many things to deal with was willing to take care of her.

She didn't know how to react, so she just sat there, still and worried, the image of the lonely, quiet graveyard imprinted on her mind. Neil, she thought. Oh, Neil.

Gavin took out the plates and the food. She watched as he poured two glasses of freshly squeezed lemonade from an insulated carafe, then handed her one. "Drink," he said in a gentle voice.

Lacey took a sip, let the tart liquid slide down her suddenly dry throat. "Thank you."

Then he fixed her a plate of fruit and salad. She could smell the rich vinegar and garlic from the salad dressing, could almost taste the sweetness of the strawberries and peaches. But she wasn't sure if she could eat a bite.

Gavin took a couple of grapes from a

171

plastic container, then offered her one. She reached out to take it, but he held it back. "No. Let me." He held the ripe, green grape to her lips. "Go ahead."

Lacey took the grape from his fingers, wondered how she was supposed to chew. She tried to find a prayer, tried to ask God to help her through this with her heart intact, but Gavin's eyes held to hers, making her wish for forbidden things, things she had no business wishing for.

Gavin handed her her plate, then fixed one for himself. Still looking at her, he took a big bite of the salad. "Mmm. This is very good."

"Thank you," she managed to say again as she balanced her own plate on her lap. "I'm not much of a cook. Lorna is a chef — so that's her job. But everyone likes my salad dressing."

"Spicy," he said through a red-hot smile.

Spicy, Lacey thought through a burning swallow.

"Is this dressing your secret recipe?"

"Yes." She laughed nervously. "Even Lorna can't quite get it right, or at least she lets me think she doesn't know how to get it right. It's the only thing I can come up with in the kitchen, so I suppose my talented sister is just humoring me. I usually

172

make a batch and toss it on everything from pasta to steaks and it always works."

"Maybe because you make it with love in mind."

She choked on her lemonade. "Excuse me?"

"My *abuela* used to say food was better when it was made with a loving hand."

"Oh. Yes, I suppose that's true. Lorna loves to cook, and everything she makes is good."

"But you'd rather be in your shop with your antiques?"

"I enjoy cooking, even if I'm not a worldly chef like my sister," she admitted. "Or at least, I used to enjoy fixing meals for my husband." She glanced toward the cemetery again.

Gavin followed the line of her gaze. "Is he buried there?"

Lacey whirled around, unable to deny it. "Yes."

"Does this make you uncomfortable, being here with me? If so, we can go somewhere else to discuss our plans."

Should she tell him the truth, the whole truth? Lacey couldn't bring herself to do that. Instead, she put her half-eaten food down on the bench between them and got up to fold her arms over her chest to ward off the cool wind. "I don't really want to discuss anything right now."

Gavin got up, too. He took a drink of lemonade, then set his glass down on a long support beam. "Then we won't talk at all. We can go over the costumes and everything else later. In spite of your good intentions, I'm not in the mood to discuss how we're going to bring my parents to justice right now, either."

"I'm sorry, Gavin," she said. "This is hard on you, isn't it?"

His eyes went black. "*Sí*. It's too ugly to ruin a beautiful lunch. How about we dance instead?"

She gave him a surprised look. "But there's no music."

Gavin reached for her hand, forced her to drop her arms away from her body. "Yes, there is," he told her. "Listen."

Lacey went into his arms and let him lead her around the dirt-floored interior of the shaded arbor. She listened, hearing the sounds of their breathing, hearing the cool autumn wind playing through the trees, hearing the birds singing their praises to God and nature, hearing her own heart opening in a song of hope and longing.

At the other end of the long arbor, a set of butterfly-shaped pewter wind chimes danced and fluttered in the breeze.

Gavin heard them, inclined his head toward the sound. "I like the chimes."

"My brother," she tried to explain. "He has a thing for bells and chimes. He's hung them all over the property."

"Smart, romantic man. They lend themselves very nicely to the music."

"There is no music," she repeated, more to convince herself than to stop him from drawing her closer.

"Don't you hear it?" Gavin asked, his breath fanning her throat as he held her close. "Don't you hear the music of your garden, Lacey?"

How could she not? All the sights and sounds of familiar things, things she'd been around all her life, seemed to intensify and take on new meaning in her head as she leaned against Gavin's wounded shoulder and breathed in the scent of spice and soap. How long had it been, she wondered, since she'd stopped to really listen to life?

She felt a strange tingling in her stomach, standing there in Gavin's arms. She felt her world tilt and change in the stillness of the countryside. And she saw things in a different light.

"I do," she said, finally and with a finality that echoed her tortured thoughts.

Then she lifted her head so she could see his face. He looked dark and dangerous, his face cast between sun-dappled shadows and the emerging dark clouds behind him. And he was so close. Too close.

He leaned toward her, his eyes never leaving hers, his hands holding her in the center of her back as he tugged her forward. Then he lowered his mouth to hers in a soft, slow kiss that tasted of lemons and grapes.

Lacey fell against him, the music surrounding her in a flurry of melodies and ballads that touched her soul and left her longing and wanting. She wanted to dance in his arms forever.

But then she opened her eyes and remembered coming out of the chapel with Neil, remembered the bright hope of that glorious spring day. And remembered that her heart had broken into a million pieces when she'd lost both her husband and their child.

She pulled away.

Off over the trees, the clouds darkened to a deep gray as they puffed toward them, and the roar of thunder boomed like a bass drum, effectively stopping whatever melody she'd heard in her head.

She stepped back from Gavin, held a

hand to her mouth as she cried out in pain. Then she ran out of the arbor, ran toward the cemetery where her heart had been buried.

She couldn't do this. She couldn't face these feelings, not here, not in this place. This had been wrong from the beginning. It had been wrong to come here with Gavin.

Then why did you do it? the voice in her head cried out.

Lacey couldn't answer that voice. She kept running until she was inside the creaky low white gate, until she was standing in front of her husband's grave.

And the tiny grave that lay beside it.

Gavin felt the first drops of rain as he stalked after Lacey. The weather, just like her mood, had turned ominous.

He shouldn't have pushed her, he told himself as he walked toward the open gate of the small cemetery. He should have stayed away from her, should have stayed up at the house working at the computer. His life was falling apart, piece by piece, and all he could think about was the woman standing in the cemetery.

Too late to turn back now. Ignoring the mist of rain and the dark clouds blocking out the sun, he edged his way into the cemetery, noting the centuries of Dorsettes and other relatives buried there.

It was very old. Four giant, gnarled live oaks held watch over it from each corner. Crape myrtles dotted the flat landscape, peppered between the many headstones and the weathered, aboveground stone mausoleum tombs for which Louisiana was so famous.

The wind picked up, causing rustling leaves to lift in chilling, swirling circles all around Lacey.

She stood there, her arms wrapped around her waist as if to hold herself in check. She was crying.

Gavin couldn't bear her tears. But they fell as softly and surely as the rain coming down.

"Lacey, come back under the arbor," he said in a gentle voice as he wrapped her forgotten sweater around her shoulders. "It's cold and raining."

She didn't speak. Just stood there looking down, little shivers racking her body.

Gavin walked up behind her, hating the way his whole being was drawn to the man buried at her feet.

Neil Lancaster York.

"He was so young," Gavin managed to say. Then wished the earth would just swallow him up. Of course Neil had died too young. His lovely, still-young, still-grieving wife was proof of that.

"He was a good man," Lacey finally said, her voice shaky and raw with emotion. "I need to remember that."

The rain picked up, blowing in fine gray sheets now.

"Lacey, let's go home. You don't need to be out in this storm. And neither of us is in the mood for this right now."

She shrugged, held her arms tighter to her midsection. "You know, sometimes it seems as if my whole life has been one big storm. I lost my parents during a storm. Neil's plane went down during a storm. We've been through tornadoes, floods, rains, winds. Does it ever end, Gavin?"

He wanted to bring her in out of the storm. But he was trapped. He couldn't offer her the life she deserved. He didn't know how to offer her hope, either. He felt the old familiar darkness pulling at his soul, torturing him with doubt and despair.

He came to stand behind her, to tug her body back against his as he gazed down at her husband's grave. "Lacey, I don't know how to answer that question. You're the one with the crystal-clear faith. Why don't you tell me?"

"Faith?" She echoed the word as she held her head down, the tears misting her face as the rain misted her hair and clothes. "I go to church in that tiny building each Sunday. I walk around pretending that I'm close to God. But right now I feel as if I've let God down. I feel as if my faith has been a sham."

Gavin kissed the back of her head. "Don't say that, *bella*. Don't even think it. You are . . . an example of what faith is all about. You didn't turn away from God, even in the darkest times. I wish I could say the same."

She turned to face him then, and Gavin would remember until his dying days the anguish in her blue eyes. "Oh, I've questioned God many, many times, Gavin. I've doubted and wondered and . . . I've had this bitter silence in my heart. I didn't realize how bitter I truly was until Lorna and Lucas both found happiness. I resented my own sister and brother for finding the very things I had already known. What kind of faith is that?"

"An honest one," he told her, his hands stroking her damp hair. "Let me take you away from here. Let's go back to the arbor. Or we can hurry back home if you want."

She lowered her head onto his shoulder, her sobs coming faster now. "I want . . . I want to understand. I want to know if God brought us together, or if this is some kind of test, some sort of cruel twist of fate."

Gavin held her in his arms, his gaze moving around the dark and gloomy cemetery. There didn't seem to be any way out of this. He and Lacey were caught up in something unpredictable, something both amazing and scary. And he didn't have a clue as to what the outcome would be.

He looked down, a prayer to the God he'd ignored for so long forming in his head.

And then he saw another grave beside her husband's.

A tiny pearl-tinged bit of marble with an etching of a cherub on it.

Baby Christopher Lance York. Stillborn child of Lacey Dorsette York and Neil Lancaster York.

And he at last understood the true measure of Lacey's grief. And why she sometimes doubted the God in whom she so believed.

Somehow, Gavin guided her from the

grave site back under the shelter of the arbor. They were both soaked and chilled to the bone, but he didn't push her to go home just yet. Instead, he urged her down on the bench and into his arms. And there he let her cry out the rest of her tears while he held her.

The rainstorm turned gentle. Its soft, dripping cadence filled the quiet countryside, and colored the whole world in a deeper shade of autumn.

Gavin held Lacey tightly to his chest, his gaze wandering back to the cemetery. It looked forlorn and sad there in the misting rain. He had to close his eyes to what he'd seen there. But he couldn't close his heart to the woman in his arms. It wasn't possible, like not breathing, not feeling.

But there were just too many obstacles between them right now for anything other than this brief time together, in spite of his need to protect her forever.

"Lacey," he said, his voice low. "Lacey, I saw the other grave."

She didn't lift her head. "Lance," she said into his damp shirt. "We were going to call him Lance. Another name beginning with *L*, just to keep tradition, you understand."

"It's a good name." What else did you

say to a grieving mother who'd lost a child at birth?

"He would have been a good boy." She shifted in his arms, as if burrowing closer for warmth. "He . . . I had a miscarriage when I was five months pregnant — close to six months, so close." Her voice went so low, Gavin had to lean his head down in order to hear her. "I got to hold him in my arms for such a little while. They . . . didn't want to let me, didn't want me to remember him that way. But I remember the beauty in that tiny body. That's what I remember."

Gavin let out a breath, then stroked her hair away from her tearstained face. "*Lo siento.* I'm so sorry for your loss, Lacey. So sorry."

The words weren't nearly enough, he knew. And holding her close to his heart wasn't enough, either. Gavin didn't know how to deal with this kind of pain, this soul-deep sorrow. Her sorrow was guilt ridden and full of loneliness.

And his presence here had only added to that burden.

But Gavin wouldn't bring that point up now. Instead he let her talk. She told him about her wedding right here in the chapel. Told him about how she'd traveled with

Neil, how she'd relished being an officer's wife. She smiled through her tears when she remembered finding out she was going to have a baby. Neil was away on temporary duty, but when he came back home that autumn, they celebrated together. Then, in her third month of the pregnancy, Neil had to go back. And his plane went down during a training mission.

"I tried to stay strong," she said. "I tried to keep up my strength for the baby's sake. But I missed Neil so much. Everyone went out of their way to take care of me — Aunt Hilda, Lorna and Lucas. All the neighbors and our friends." She looked up at him, her eyes wide, her tears wet against her face. "But . . . I didn't do so well. I lost the baby. Gavin, I lost the baby. It's my fault. All my fault."

A silent rage swept over Gavin. "No, *bella,* no. It wasn't your fault. It wasn't."

He could see it all so clearly now. How she'd been carrying this burden for so long. How she must have come here to this place day after day, standing there over those graves, her guilt and her shame surrounding her like a shroud. No wonder she had retreated from the world.

He wanted to help her, wanted to bring her back to the world that needed her gentleness and her goodness so much. But he didn't know if he was the one capable of doing that. Didn't know if he deserved such a challenge and such an honor.

But he did know one thing. Lacey liked to stay busy. That was how she handled the pain, the grief. If he could keep her busy until the end of the week, until he could leave and know she was safe, his conscience would be absolved a little bit, at least.

He held her for a long time, until long after the rain had gone and a cool mist was all that was left in its wake. He let her cry, let her talk, let her rest.

And then he decided he had only one option left. Gavin had to get Lacey back away from the brink of that dark pain he'd seen in her shining eyes today.

So he lifted her head, touched a finger to her tears and told her, "I . . . haven't been honest with you." That statement made her eyes clear, but his next one made them go misty again. "I do need your help, Lacey. We need to get busy. You're supposed to help me design an outfit for the costume ball, remember?"

She nodded. "I remember." Then she sat up, her expression almost no-nonsense again. "I'm sorry I spoiled our picnic."

Gavin ran a finger down the length of her cheekbone. "You didn't spoil anything. I shouldn't have kissed you. I should have respected your memories and your grief."

She got up to gather their things. "I don't know why I brought you here. Except . . . it's the one place where I can be alone with my thoughts, where I feel close to the Lord and my husband and child. I come here a lot."

So you can sit and blame yourself, he thought.

"Maybe you wanted to tell me, but didn't know how to go about it — I mean about the baby and everything you've been through."

"Well, now you know all of it," she responded. "I guess I accomplished that much, at least."

That, and taking my heart, Gavin thought. But he couldn't tell her that. Not yet.

He hadn't forgotten his earlier promise, however.

Somehow, he'd make things right and he'd come back here with Lacey. He'd like to believe that on that day, he'd be the one walking her down the aisle in the Chapel in the Garden. But that dream seemed as dark and misty as the surrounding countryside. It was more of an illusion, an unattainable, unreachable illusion, best left far in the recesses of his mind.

But he would come back. And he'd make her forget her grief and her guilt.

And maybe he'd find absolution and the redeeming love of Christ for himself in the process.

Chapter Eleven

"So, our plan is complete?"

Lacey nodded at Gavin's question. It was late and she looked exhausted. They'd spent the better part of the day working, she on their costumes and he on what to do once they got into the ball.

And they'd spent the better part of their time trying to avoid the undercurrents and unanswered questions swirling like the stormy weather all around them.

It didn't help that they'd had to touch each other as they tried on their costumes, buttoning and zipping here and there. It didn't help that she'd looked like something out of a dream in her shimmering golden gown with the ruffles and tufts. Lacey was a beauty in any century.

She'd made elaborate masks from silk and paper, with materials and feathers to hide their faces, and maybe to hide their real feelings for each other.

"Okay, then." Gavin checked the boxes once more, already sorry that he'd have to leave her behind. "The rain's stopped for now. I'm going to put everything we need into your car —"

"Let's take the SUV," Lacey interrupted. Before he could question, she added, "Different vehicle. Faster getaway. And with this weather, it'll make driving easier, too."

That broke some of the tension and only reinforced Gavin's concerns. "You are a quick study, Lacey."

"I'm learning," she said, her words flat and dull.

Gavin hated seeing her this way, hated knowing that he was the cause of her stress and her guilt. She'd been almost listless since yesterday, since the picnic in the grape arbor. Wishing he could find a way to bring back the prim, proper, teasing Lacey he'd come to know, he grabbed up their equipment and started for the back door.

"You'll need the key," Lacey said, rushing across the kitchen to a small key cabinet. "The SUV is in the garage down by the side entry lane. The black Yukon parked by Lucas's Jeep."

"I'll find it."

"You've got everything, right? The laptop, that other fancy little spying gadget the delivery man brought, and your cell phone?"

"Got it all," he replied. And they'd gone

189

over the details countless times. Though Lacey wouldn't be with him, she had no way of knowing that, so Gavin had been forced to come up with two plans — one that included her and the real one that wouldn't. "I'll pay you back for footing the bill."

"The shop footed the bill. And the delivery man is used to dropping off strange packages, so we should be clear there, too."

"*Sí,* all clear." Hearing another roar of thunder, he added, "And let's hope that tropical storm down in the Gulf veers away from New Orleans."

She gripped the keys. "If this storm turns into a full-blown hurricane, it might be hard to get back into the city."

"I know. And right here at the very end of hurricane season, too. Just another small problem to have to overcome." But he'd do it. He'd swim into New Orleans if he had to. He wanted this over and done, storm or no storm.

He lifted the hefty box, then turned to tilt it against a kitchen counter. "Lacey, when I get back . . . I think we need to talk."

"Of course. You'll want to go over everything once more, just to be sure."

Gavin didn't tell her that there was only

190

one thing he needed to be sure about —
her. He was worried about her frame of
mind, about her mood. They'd both been
brooding, just like the unpredictable
weather. But he aimed to put a stop to
Lacey's worries, at least.

He'd been bad for her from the beginning, dragging her along on this dangerous
mission, dragging her nurturing heart into
his dark, misguided world. He wanted her
safe again. He wanted her to know she
didn't have to feel guilty because of him.

"I'll be back in a few minutes," he said.
"Will you be okay here?"

"I'll be fine. Just going to clear away our
coffee cups and dessert dishes, then call it
a night."

Gavin hefted the box up and started out
the door. Then froze. "Lacey, there's a car
coming up the drive."

Lacey rushed to the back gallery.
Squinting into the darkness, she let out a
groan. "Oh, that looks like Justin's car."

"Justin, your landscaper friend?"

"Yes." Turning to Gavin, she pushed him
forward. "Go. Get out of here. You can get
to the SUV and stay there in the garage
until he's gone."

"And just how long do you think that
might be?"

Lacey shrugged, clutched her pearls. "I don't know. Justin can linger over the simplest of topics sometimes. Just go, Gavin. I'll come down and find you after I've visited with him a bit."

"Which way?"

The white car halted at the end of the graveled drive. They heard a door bang shut. "Take the path down by the summerhouse, then on to the restaurant. Keep going, following the bayou. You'll come to the garage sitting up on the slope."

Gavin nodded, started walking. "If you don't come for me in a few minutes, I'm coming back up here to make sure everything is all right."

"Okay, go, go," she said as footsteps echoed over the path toward the gallery. "Get out of here before he sees you."

Gavin lugged his box out another door, then hid in the shadow of one of the great oaks, listening and watching.

"Justin, you're back early," he heard Lacey say, her voice almost too surprised and cheerful. "What brings you out here so late?"

"I was worried about you," the red-headed, slender man said.

"Me, I'm fine, just fine," Lacey said as she ushered him into the kitchen.

Gavin saw her turn and look out into the night.

And knew she was searching for him.

"You really should go up to New England with me sometime, Lacey," Justin said as he bit into another slice of sweet-potato pie. "Mmm. Even after being frozen and reheated, Lorna's pie is still the best."

"More coffee?" Lacey asked, nervously glancing at the big clock on the wall behind Justin's head. He'd been chattering away about his recent trip for well over twenty minutes.

"Maybe half a cup." Justin finished his pie, then settled back to rub his stomach. "I sure missed Lorna's and Rosie Lee's cooking."

"Now, Justin, they have wonderful food up north. Surely you tried some clam chowder and Boston brown bread."

"Yep, but there is no food like Louisiana food. You should know that."

"You're right, of course." Lacey hopped up, sure she'd heard a noise outside the open doors. Stifling a yawn, she poured Justin some fresh coffee. "I'd love to travel up north one day, but . . . I just can't seem to find the time."

Justin poked his fork into the air. "You

see, that's exactly why I came out to check on you. Saw Josh and Kathryn at the new general store in Jardin and they said you'd been so busy they hadn't even heard from you. They were worried about you out here all by yourself."

Feeling remorseful for not calling her friends, Lacey started clearing away dishes. "Well, I was in New Orleans last weekend, as they both knew. I got back here early to do some work in the shop. I got so caught up, I just didn't think to call."

"That's what I mean. And that's why I called Lucas."

Lacey looked down at the man sitting at the table. "You called Lucas in Europe, just to check up on *me?*"

"No. He and Willa are back in the States. In New York, visiting her parents."

"Oh, really. I didn't know that."

"That's because you haven't checked the messages on the answering machine or read your e-mail, obviously. Kathryn knew Lucas and Willa were winding their way home, knew Aunt Hilda's whereabouts, even talked to Lorna — who's just as worried about you, by the way."

Lacey let out a long sigh, her eyes still on the clock. "Don't tell me you called Lorna, too?"

"No, but Kathryn did. Lorna said you didn't seem yourself the other day."

Holding tightly to what little patience she had left, Lacey retorted, "No, I think that was the other way around. Lorna was having a fit of worries, and I tried to comfort her. You know, that's what I do, Justin. I comfort, I nurture, I try really hard to take care of everyone around here."

Justin jumped up so fast, the high-backed chair he'd been sitting in almost tipped over. Steadying it with a freckled hand, he glanced across the table at Lacey. "Hey, we all know that. That's why we're worried. Why you insisted on staying here alone is beyond me, but I'm back now and I'm going to take care of you for a change."

In spite of her irritation, Lacey couldn't help but be touched by his sweetness. That was Justin, sweet, overprotective, almost annoying in the way he hovered and watched over her. Standing there, seeing the genuine concern on his face, Lacey wished she could find some feelings for Justin other than friendship. Lorna had often told her that the man was head over heels in love with her, but Lacey had refused to see it.

Tonight she saw it, plain and clear.

And knew she could never return that love.

Especially not now, not when Gavin was out there in the dark somewhere. Still feeling raw and guilt ridden about her feelings toward Gavin only made her that much more determined to keep her head clear.

"Feast or famine," she said out loud before she'd even realized it. Aunt Hilda said that was the way of love sometimes.

"What?" Justin shot her a puzzled look, then came around the table. "Lacey, you shouldn't be alone. Lorna reminded me — it's close to the anniversary of Neil's death."

"I know that," she said, agitation making her words harsh. "And I really wish everyone would just respect that and leave me to a little bit of private grief."

"Is that what you want?" Justin asked, his green eyes bright with pain and concern. "Do you want to be here all alone, remembering what you went through?"

"Alone or in a crowd, it's there, Justin," she said sincerely. Then because she knew he was only trying to help, she added, "But I appreciate your thoughtfulness. And it's good to have you home."

"Want to go for a walk or something?"

196

She heard it again. The rustling in the hedges. Gavin, no doubt. If she didn't get Justin out of here soon, Gavin would come rushing in like a gallant knight, bent on protecting her. But from what? Justin was harmless.

"No," she said in answer to Justin's question. "I think I just want to get some sleep. It's been a long day and I'm so tired."

"Of course you are. Just wanted to see you, make sure you were okay."

"I'm perfectly fine." She started toward the door, hoping Justin would follow suit.

He walked with her, slow and steady. "I'll be around tomorrow. The wet ground's gonna halt things, but I can do some pruning here and there, get some of the bulbs and perennials ready for winter."

Lacey's heart raced at that statement. How was she supposed to keep Justin from finding out about Gavin?

"Of course," she said as she watched him down the path. "But you still have vacation coming until Monday."

"I won't do much. Just see the lay of the land."

The lay of the land was different now, she wanted to tell him. But she wouldn't lie to Justin. Suddenly, however, this game of espionage wasn't so fun anymore.

"Well, I guess I'll see you then," she said, unsure how to handle this situation.

"We could have breakfast together," Justin said hopefully.

"I'd planned an early start at the shop."

"Okay." He shrugged, then gave her a hangdog look of disappointment. "See you later, then."

"Yes. Good night, Justin."

She waited there on the gallery in the chilly, damp night wind, leaning against an aged column, until she saw the taillights of his white sedan exiting through the remote-control gate. As she turned to go back in, Lacey felt an arm go around her waist.

Letting out a gasp, she glanced around to see Gavin's face. "Gavin, you scared me."

"Sorry, *querida*." He pulled her body back against his, his whisper warm in her ear. "But I think your friend Justin is going to be a problem for us."

"Let me handle Justin."

"I'm only trying to protect both of you, Lacey. If he finds me here, he will be in danger, too."

"Then maybe we'd better leave early — tonight?"

"That's a thought," he said as he whirled

her around and held her in his arms. "But we'd be safer here than in New Orleans a day early. We could hide, but it would be risky."

"Then you'll just have to stay in the house, out of Justin's way."

"Hard to do, since the man promises to pop in and out — to check on you, of course."

"He's just being kind."

"He's in love with you."

She looked up at Gavin's dark eyes, wondering if she saw jealousy there, then chided herself for even thinking it. "And how do you know that? Were you listening to our conversation?"

"Enough to see that the man has a bad case of . . . *estar enamorado* . . . he's enamored of you. And that could make him dangerous."

"Justin Hayes, dangerous? That's ridiculous. Justin is a decent, hardworking man and a dear friend." But she felt a shiver and it wasn't from the cold.

"Who will do whatever it takes to protect you."

"And why do you think it will come to that, to Justin having to protect me, I mean?"

His eyes were black now. And she reminded herself yet again that *he* was the dangerous one. And the one to whom she was inexplicably drawn.

"Lacey, any number of things could go wrong between now and the night of the ball. Justin just complicates matters."

She tried to pull away, but he held her there. She stayed because he was so very warm and inviting. "I don't see how things can get any more complicated, Gavin."

"Sí." He lifted his head, his spiked, inky-black hair almost covering his dark brows as the brisk wind played through it. *"Complicado,* is true," he said, his accent thickening as he leaned close. *"We* are complicated. I am a problem for you, because you can't decide how you feel about me, no?"

Her breath hitched. "I was talking about . . . what brought us together. You're on the run, in trouble, doing dangerous deeds in the dead of night, remember? That makes all of it a problem."

In spite of the clouds shifting to cover the pale moon, she saw regret there in his dark eyes. "I told you I was a bad boy."

That brought her chin up, made her defiant. "You might have been a bad boy, Gavin. But I believe you are a good man now."

"But a man you don't want to be attracted to, right?"

She lowered her head again, closed her eyes.

Gavin forced her chin back up, his hand cupping it. "You can't even admit it, can't even look me in the eye."

Lacey was too honest to deny what was in her heart. "Yes, I am attracted to you, but yesterday, in the arbor, I realized that it's wrong. Very wrong."

"Because I'm such a bad boy?"

"No."

"Because you can't let go of what might have been . . . with your husband and your child?"

"Yes," she said. "Yes."

He released her, then turned to brush a hand over his hair. Then he leaned into the column opposite the one to which she'd been clinging. "Complicated," he said again. Then he turned and walked away.

Frustrated, Lacey stared out into the shadowy garden. The wet night smelled fresh and crisp, like newly washed linens. The earth here was ancient and rich, gleaned from a million fallen leaves, from the roots of the sturdy trees that had flourished through time and nature. And gleaned from the love and tender care of her family and the people who loved this land.

Turn to the gardens, she heard Aunt Hilda's sweet voice saying. *Turn to the Lord.*

Lacey wished for the comfort of her aunt's arms right now. Aunt Hilda would advise her, tell her to follow her heart and trust in God's grace.

Lacey looked up, saw Gavin standing underneath the same oak he'd stood by his first night here. She somehow knew without seeing that he was touching a finger to his cross necklace. Maybe he was praying, too. Maybe he was asking God to show him the way through all of this.

Can it be wrong? she thought. Is it wrong to have these feelings for him? He's so different from Neil. He's . . . like a whole new awakening. A new love.

And that was it, she realized. That was what was making her so afraid and so guilty. Gavin made her feel things she'd never felt with Neil. She'd always love Neil, always treasure him in her heart. But these feelings, these emotions she'd experienced since meeting Gavin — they were very overpowering and overwhelming. And very real.

How could she deny that?

Without hesitation, without thinking

about yesterday or tomorrow, she went to Gavin. To tell him that she believed in his goodness, his kindness, his redemption.

Even if she couldn't let go of the past enough to share a future with him.

Gavin looked up as she ran through the wet night. Without a word, he opened his arms and pulled her close, cradling her in his embrace. Then he kissed her, his hands pulling through her hair, his whispers touching on her skin as he spoke soft, sweet words into her ear. Beautiful Spanish words, endearing words, comforting words.

"Usted es me corazón."

No matter the language, Lacey understood. She understood. And she felt her heart lifting out into the night . . . toward this man. She wrapped her arms around his broad back and pulled her hands through his dark hair so she could kiss him again.

Gavin held her there, underneath the great old oak tree, and for a brief time she belonged only to him.

Chapter Twelve

It would be only him. He'd gone over and over the details in his mind, and Gavin was determined to do this on his own, his own way. He had all the equipment programmed and set up to encrypt anything he downloaded or stored on the new laptop. It would literally take an act of Congress for even the FBI to get to his files now.

He also had the proper equipment to unerase any shredded hard drive files on the computer system in his father's oversize Lake Pontchartrain mansion. He knew the files had been hidden so deeply inside the senator's elaborate private system, they'd be hard to find. But Gavin knew each and every way there was to find a computer file. Even one that had supposedly been deleted. And what he didn't know, his old friend Harry was ready and willing to deliver. The trick was to get in and get the job done before the senator's well-paid cronies hid or destroyed the data completely.

There would be password protections to get through, shredded data to find and piece back together, but if he just had a few minutes alone in his father's office, Gavin knew he could find the codes and thus the money trail. There had to be some slack space in the hard drive. Gavin would find it.

Unable to sleep, he'd told Lacey goodnight before coming into the office to scan and scour all the files he could reach and download with the state-of-the-art laptop. He'd found his own — they seemed to be safe and secure, but that could be deceiving. And he had to be careful of entering them. He'd encrypted them all under a new code, had used a back-door entry, had been careful that he couldn't be traced. If he lost his laptop, he could access everything from the cell phone, and he could easily relocate the laptop with the tracking device he'd also installed. It would beep loudly enough for him to find the laptop, even with the mansion crowded with guests for the ball. But if that happened, it would be just a matter of time before the FBI figured it out, or before his father nailed him.

He stopped for a minute to glance up at the clock in the tiny room off the kitchen. It was almost dawn. The rain had returned, falling softly against the brown-tinged magnolia leaves just outside the window. It was getting colder outside, too.

He touched a hand to the heavy cross hanging around his neck and thought of Lacey. He thought of how she'd come to him there in the garden, how she'd rushed headlong into his open, waiting arms. How could she have known that Gavin had been standing there, holding this very cross, praying to the God he'd so often taken for granted?

Praying for a way out. For both Lacey and himself. Praying for guidance, and the strength to walk away from her, to do the things he had to do to find his honor again, to find his soul again.

He'd been standing there in her garden, praying to her God, his God, when she'd come to him.

Gavin had been so overwhelmed, he could do nothing but take her in his arms and try to tell her how he was feeling. He'd spoken in Spanish. Did she know that he'd told her she was his heart, that he would come back to her someday?

Before the sun came up, he'd leave her. Tomorrow this special place would be just a memory. The touch of her lips to his would be just a memory. The way she felt in his arms would be just a memory.

He'd kissed her one last time at the door of her room. And without words they had conveyed what they had been feeling since the day they'd met. He'd wanted to tell her so many things, and yet he'd only kissed her and told her good-night.

Now everything was ready. He'd done all he could from here. He was going to New Orleans today, before Justin came back and found him here. He'd wait until the right time to enter the heavily guarded, heavily decorated estate of Senator Edward Prescott. Gavin was going to march in there and take back everything the senator had taken from him.

Silently he packed the rest of his equipment inside the black duffel bag with the laptop, then checked the CDs and disks he'd need to download all the evidence, and made sure the cell phone was on and operating. Then he went into the kitchen to look around.

The big room was dark, but still warm and inviting. A single light glittered over the huge industrial stove. The refrigerator hummed, the cabinets and countertops glimmered and gleamed. A clay pot of yellow and white mums graced the center of the long breakfast table.

Gavin would miss this kitchen, this house.

He carefully unlocked the French doors, as silent and stealthy as he used to be when he'd sneak away from his room and roam the streets of New Orleans.

This was it.

He hefted the square-shaped bag's sturdy strap over one shoulder, turned to take one last look at the kitchen, then pivoted to leave before he changed his mind.

And was greeted with an iron-hard hand grabbing him around the throat, and a carefully controlled whisper near his ear. "I don't know who you are, pal, or what you're doing in my kitchen, but you're not going anywhere until I get some answers."

Gavin tried to find his breath as he stared into the face of the black-eyed, raven-haired, very angry man holding him back against the glass-paned door. Telling himself to stay cool, for Lacey's sake, he kept his own expression blank and tried to speak. "Can't —"

"Can't talk?" the man asked, releasing his hold just enough to give Gavin some much-needed air. "How's that, better, *oui?*"

Recognition hit Gavin even as the first

precious breath swept through his lungs. "Lucas?"

The man gave him a skeptical look of surprise. "How do you know my name, man?"

Relief swept over Gavin. He had not been looking forward to a fistfight before he got out of here. "Lacey . . . talks about you all the time."

That brought Lucas Dorsette's strong hand back to his throat. "And what would you know about my sister?"

With an equally effective grip, Gavin brought his free hand up to grab Lucas's arms, then stood nose-to-nose with Lacey's angry brother. "If you'll let me go, I'll tell you everything I know."

Lucas glared at him a full minute. Gavin held his ground, knowing that first impressions made lasting impressions. And knowing that he was going to have to do some fancy maneuvering to get out of here before Lacey discovered him in a tussle with her overly protective brother.

Finally, with a snarl, Lucas shoved him back into the dark kitchen, then closed the door with a booted foot. "Start talking."

Gavin set the duffel bag down on the counter, then ran a hand through his hair. "It's a long story."

Lucas circled him in a slow, lazy observation. "Me, I got plenty of time. You, on the other hand, *mon ami,* your time is running out."

Gavin held his hands up. "Okay. I met Lacey in New Orleans —"

"And followed her home?"

How to play this? "She invited me here," Gavin said, nodding.

Lucas grinned, then folded his arms across his chest as he leaned back against the opposite counter. "Lacey invited you? My Lacey?"

"Your Lacey," Gavin said, noting that the sun was coming up and that pesky Justin might be arriving any minute. He had to get out of here soon, or all the men in Lacey's life would be ganging up on him.

Lucas shook his head, then wagged a finger. "Now, you see, that just doesn't sound like the Lacey I know and love. And besides, if she invited you here why are you trying so hard to sneak out at the crack of dawn?"

Gavin shrugged, laughed. "You got me there. I have to get back to New Orleans and I didn't want to wake Lacey."

The amused expression on Lucas's face changed like a bolt of lightning crossing the swamp. "And just how are things between you and Lacey, anyway? Just exactly how close are you and my sister, that she'd invite you back here?"

Growing impatient now, Gavin let out a sigh of frustration. "Look, like I said, it's a long story and I really need to get going now. I will tell you that your sister's honor is safe. I've been a gentleman in every regard. Lacey can fill you in on all the details, if she wants to."

"No, no." Lucas dropped his hands to his side, shot Gavin a wry grin. "I'd rather hear it from you — gentleman to gentleman."

Gavin decided to tell it straight. "I can't explain right now, but I have to get out of here. I have to get back to New Orleans today. So you need to let me go. It's for Lacey's sake. I have to leave before she wakes up."

Lucas pursed his lips, shot Gavin a look of disdain. "Oh, it's that way, *hein?* Love her and leave her?"

Gavin decided he might just welcome that fistfight after all. "You've got it all wrong, Lucas. Lacey has been very kind to me. She's helped me with some . . . business problems."

"Oh, and what kind of business are you in, exactly?"

"I'm a lawyer."

"Really. Mind telling me your name, then, since you know mine?"

Gavin lowered his head, tried to count to ten. Lucas had been out of the country, so it was possible that he hadn't heard the local news. "It's Prescott. Gavin Prescott."

Lucas held a finger to his chin, as if he were deep in thought. "Prescott. That name sounds familiar."

"It's a common American name."

"Yeah, but you're more of a Hispanic descent, if I pegged your accent, right?"

"I am," Gavin replied, not giving away any more than he had to.

Lucas inched forward. "Okay, Mr. Latino. I don't buy the name. And I don't buy your story. It looks to me like you might be trying to make a fast getaway with the heirloom silver. What's in the duffel bag, anyway?"

"My laptop," Gavin said, eyeing the black canvas bag he'd laid on the counter. "I do have work to do."

"And in such a hurry to get it done."

Gavin prepared himself. He was going to grab the duffel bag and rush at Lucas, hitting him just hard enough to knock him down. Then he was going to run. It was the only choice he had.

But first he'd give Lacey's brother fair warning. "I'm leaving now." He edged toward the bag. "I don't want any trouble. But I'm going to leave."

"Right." Lucas watched him with a steady determination.

Gavin had to give him credit. The man was as tenacious as a gator stalking its quarry. He could understand Lucas's need to protect Lacey, though. He felt that same need. Which was why he was going to have to knock out her brother right now.

He lunged for the small duffel bag right as Lucas lunged for him. With a grunt, Gavin got to the bag, then shoved it right into Lucas's rock-hard gut. Winded but not down, Lucas growled and backed against the counter while Gavin headed for the door.

Lucas slammed into Gavin's back, dragging him against the door enough to cause the panes to rattle. The door came open and they both fell with a loud thud out onto the brick floor of the gallery. The duffel bag went flying as the two men, equal in size, rolled and struggled together, each throwing punches.

And that's how Lacey found them.

At first her heart went into a tailspin. Someone had Gavin down on the ground, trying to strangle him!

Grabbing a large cast-iron frying pan, Lacey rushed out onto the porch, prepared to hit the attacker squarely on the head. Until she saw the dark head and recognized the familiar shouts of some choice Cajun slang words.

"Lucas," she screamed. "Lucas, let him up! Lucas?"

Her brother glanced back, but didn't answer. And didn't stop his attack. But Gavin took the slight inclination of Lucas's head as a second of advantage, whirling with both hands on Lucas's arms so he could flip the other man over and pin him down. Briefly. Before Lucas grunted and tried to force Gavin off, using the tried-and-true strangulation technique that seemed to be his specialty.

"Lucas Dorsette," Lacey shouted, "don't make me have to use this frying pan. I said let him go!"

Some of the rage left Lucas's flushed face as he pulled his hands away from Gavin's throat. Still wary, Gavin kept Lucas pinned there in the mud and dirt just off the porch floor, then looked over his shoulder to find Lacey standing there in a blue flowing robe with a frying pan raised over her head.

214

Heaving a breath, Gavin lifted himself up, bringing the still-fuming Lucas with him to a sitting position. Gulping several much-needed breaths, he said, "Your brother is one hotheaded hombre."

"Tell me about it," Lacey said, glaring down at Lucas.

He glared right back, his gaze shifting from her to Gavin. "Well, what am I supposed to think? I get a call from Lorna, followed by a call from Aunt Hilda, followed by yet another call from Justin, telling me that something strange is going on. Mimi called Kathryn and told her your town house in New Orleans had been ransacked, and because Kathryn didn't want to upset *you*, and because Justin had told Kathryn that *you* didn't want any calls, she called *me* first. I tell you, it's hard to have a honeymoon with this family always interrupting! I left Willa with her parents and took the red-eye home, parked down by the bayou so I could check things out — only to find this . . . *lawyer* lurking about in my kitchen at five o'clock in the morning. And I haven't even had a decent cup of coffee yet!"

He said more, but he lapsed into Cajun French. Gavin got the impression he really didn't want to hear this part, anyway.

Finally Lucas stopped ranting and shoved a hand at the arm Gavin still held to his. "Get away from me."

"Gladly," Gavin said, rising off the wet ground. He had mud all over him and he hurt, especially in his wounded shoulder.

Lucas stayed on the ground, his knees up, his hands hanging palm-down over them. "Don't go anywhere," he told Gavin. "I mean, I know you were in an all-fired hurry to get out of here this morning, but . . . you've still got some explaining to do."

Lacey looked from her brother to Gavin, shock and realization colliding inside her stomach. "Yes, you certainly do. Gavin, were you going to go to New Orleans without me?"

Gavin sent Lucas a heated gaze, but remained silent. Lacey's heart sank. He couldn't even face her. Which meant he'd been planning on leaving, all right. "You were, weren't you?" she said, her eyes misting. But she refused to cry. And she didn't understand why his betrayal should hurt so much.

Lucas got up then, brushing his jeans off with an elegance that bordered on arrogance. "That was the plan, sister — at least, that's all *I* could get out of him. Now, would you both like to tell me exactly what's going on, over a very strong pot of coffee?"

Gavin watched as Lacey whirled with feminine fury back into the kitchen, then said over her shoulder, "I'd like to know that myself."

"Thanks a lot," Gavin said to Lucas on a low, threatening voice.

"Anytime." Lucas gestured toward the kitchen. "She's waiting for you, pal." Then he tapped Gavin on the arm. "Hey, just a friendly warning. If you hurt my sister, you have me to answer to, understand, Don Juan?"

Gavin nodded. "When I explain things, I hope you'll understand that I'm trying very hard *not* to hurt your sister."

"I'm all ears," Lucas replied through a dark scowl.

Gavin went back inside, thinking that for a remote plantation house, this place sure was getting crowded. And the more people involved, the more danger for all of them. He wondered how he was ever going to pull this off now.

And he wondered if Lacey would ever forgive him for trying to leave her behind.

He walked up to her, reached out a hand.

"Stop it," she said, hurt and disappointment written clearly in her eyes.

"Lacey —"

"You were just going to go, without a word, without an explanation or a goodbye?"

"Yes," he said, nodding slowly. "Yes, I was."

Chapter Thirteen

Lacey put the coffee on to brew. Loudly. Banging pots and pans, she managed to scrape up some toast and jelly. Without looking at either her mud-caked brother's inquisitive eyes or Gavin's dirty brooding face, she slammed plates onto the table and slid cups down beside them.

Lucas seemed to be slightly amused, in spite of the worried looks he cast her way now and again. "You've made her mad," he pointed out to Gavin with a smirk.

"Maybe she's mad at you," Gavin countered with a scowl of his own. "You should have just minded your business."

"She is my business," Lucas replied, his dark eyes turning cool again.

Lacey had had enough. Whirling to face them at last, she held up a hand. "Would you both just stop it. I'm here, in the room. And I'm mad at *both of you*."

They started talking at once.

"Why me?" Lucas asked, surprise coloring his expression.

"You have every right to be angry at me," Gavin admitted, lowering his head.

"See. He says you should be mad at him," Lucas pointed out. "That clears me."

"No, it doesn't," she retorted, pouring his coffee very close to the brim. "You blast in here, attack a guest in our home, wrestling with him like a schoolboy —"

Lucas threw his hands in the air. "I thought the man was a thief. And . . . I was worried about you."

"And that's another thing," she said, raising her own hand. "I do so wish everyone would just quit worrying about me. If I don't want to answer the phone or talk to anyone, that's my business."

"Not when you're staying here all alone," Lucas replied, his gaze sweeping over Gavin with contempt. Then he took a long swig of coffee and closed his eyes briefly, as if savoring the moment. "Now," he said as he put his cup down, "let's hear it, Lacey. All of it."

Lacey glanced over at Gavin. He looked impatient and mad himself. Maybe because his attempt to leave her behind had been foiled. She supposed she should thank Lucas. If he hadn't shown up, Gavin would be long gone by now.

And she would have been alone, all alone, again.

Lucas drummed his fingers on the counter. "I'm waiting. I'd really like to know what our friend here is doing — or was trying to do — when I found him."

Lacey let out a long-suffering sigh. "I met Gavin in New Orleans."

"So he told me."

"Okay, then that's all you need to know."

Lucas shook his head. "Ah, *non, chère.* It's not like you to bring home strays." He said this with a look of complete disdain toward Gavin.

"He's not a stray," Lacey said, rattled and soul weary. "Look, Lucas, I can explain everything, but you have to promise that you won't get angry and attack Gavin again. I brought him here. It was my decision."

Lucas watched her, his eyebrows rising. "You're scaring me, Lacey. I have a feeling I'm not gonna like this."

Gavin got up to stare across the table at Lacey. "Just let me go, Lacey. Let me go and get this thing done. You don't need to be there."

"Is that why you were leaving so early?" she asked, ignoring her brother's confused look. "After everything we've been through, you were just going to leave without a word."

"It wasn't like that," Gavin replied, his hands braced against the table. "Can we talk privately, so I can make you see reason?"

"Hey, she can see reason right here with me in the room," Lucas said. "But me, I don't feel so reasonable and I'm beginning to think my sister is in way over her head."

"She is," Gavin told him, turning to frown at him. "I need to get back to New Orleans. And you need to convince your sister to stay here where it's safe."

Lucas ran a hand through his dark curls. "Lacey, I don't like the man, but if you're in some kind of danger, then I have to agree with him."

"I can take care of myself," Lacey said, her gaze moving between the two men. "I would have been fine with Gavin in New Orleans. Gavin just doesn't trust me." She ignored the little voice in her head that reminded her of the way he'd held her last night. She tried to ignore the way he was looking at her now with those black-hot eyes.

"That's not it, *bella*," Gavin said, his words low. "You should know that's not it."

"*Bella*, is it?" Lucas got up, shook a finger in Gavin's bruised face. "I don't think I like you speaking to my sister on such intimate terms."

Gavin shoved Lucas away with an impatient grunt, then came around the table to face Lacey. "Your sister is a lady. I respect her in every way. Which is why I was trying to spare her any more pain."

"Sounds logical to me, sister," Lucas said, his arms crossed over his chest as he watched them. Lacey felt the intensity of her brother's knowing gaze, saw the little flare of understanding in his dark eyes.

Lacey tried to stay calm. If Gavin got any closer, Lucas would see everything. He'd know she was in love with Gavin. She'd accepted that right along with the realization that he'd planned on leaving her behind.

"We need to talk," Gavin said to her, his voice low, his accent stretching like a growl.

"Lucas," she said, her eyes on Gavin, "could you leave us alone for a minute?"

"No."

"Lucas, please!"

"I still don't know what's going on," Lucas pointed out, not budging.

"I'll tell you everything if you just give us some time together," Lacey said.

"Looks to me as if you've had way too

much time together already."

Lacey let out a frustrated sigh, then gave her brother a defiant look. "Lucas, please leave the room."

With a groan, Lucas grabbed a piece of toast, placed it over the top of his cup, then took the nearly full coffeepot in the other hand. "I'll be out on the gallery nursing my split lip."

He turned to leave, but before he could reach the door, it burst open. A very pregnant Lorna entered, with her husband, Mick, carefully guiding her from behind.

"We're home!" Lorna shouted, smiling until her eyes settled on Gavin. "We came back a little early — oh, I'm sorry. I didn't know we had a guest." Then she glanced over her brother's muddy clothes and cut mouth. "Lucas, what happened to you?" Her eyes met Lacey's before she looked back at Gavin. "What's going on?"

"Come on in, Lorna. Hey, Mick!" Lucas put down the coffeepot and turned to Lacey. "Get some more cups, *bella*." He glared at Gavin as he emphasized that word. "It's going to be a long morning."

Before Lacey could move or speak, Willa breezed in through the open door, her blue-eyed gaze immediately searching out her husband. "Lucas, I was so worried.

Mother didn't like it, but I insisted on catching the next plane out right behind you, to see what was going on —"

She, too, stopped short at the sight of the mud all over Lucas and Gavin. Touching a finger to Lucas's wounded lip, she said, "You're hurt. Is everything all right?"

Lucas yanked her into his arms, crushing her in a dirt-soggy hug. "It is now that you're here. I missed you."

"We were only apart about five hours," Willa pointed out, grinning and cooing sweet nothings in his ear.

"I'm confused," Mick said, his arm around Lorna's waist as he carefully surveyed the room.

"Join the crowd," Lucas told him, holding his own wife in his arms and shooting Lorna and Mick meaningful glances as he rocked Willa gently.

Lacey could only stare at all of them. They were all here, and home way too early. Lorna and Mick. Lucas and Willa.

And Gavin.

How was she going to explain this? How would she ever be able to continue helping Gavin now?

He didn't want her help anymore, she reminded herself.

Gavin looked at the curious group, then

turned to Lacey, his angry words making his accent very pronounced. "Why don't you just go ahead and call Justin and Tía Hilda, too. And that other family — the Babineaux, *sí*, let's get them in on this, too. In fact, why don't we just alert the media and get it over with!" He continued in Spanish, rapid and animated, waving his hands in the air. "*¿Qué'mas da?* Loco! The whole situation has gone loco!"

Lacey felt the heat of his anger as her sister advanced on her with a bemused expression. Lorna leaned close, gave Lacey a hug. "He's kind of intriguing . . . and colorful. Where'd you find him?"

"In New Orleans," Lucas offered, still holding his tall, slender wife. "And she was just about to explain the whole story to me."

Lacey shot her infuriating brother a scalding look. "No, I was just about to talk to Gavin in private."

"Gavin — nice to meet you," Lorna said, extending her hand. "I'm Lorna Love, Lacey's sister."

Gavin shook her hand, his face blank, his angry eyes on Lacey. *"Haló."*

Then Lorna politely introduced the rest of them. "This is my husband, Mick, and

226

. . . I believe you've met Lucas. Here's his wife, Willa."

Gavin nodded, grunted a greeting.

"Let's just tell them," Lacey finally said. "We'll tell them . . . and then you can leave. After all, that is what you want, isn't it?"

Gavin kept his eyes on her. "You have no idea what I want right now."

Lucas chuckled, then pulled out a chair for Willa. "This is gonna be good, folks. Everybody have a seat and let's listen close while Mr. Gavin Prescott explains what he's doing here alone with our sister. And why he was trying to leave in the dark of dawn."

Cups clashed and chairs scraped across the floor while everyone started talking.

"Gavin Prescott? Related to the senator? Isn't he in some sort of political trouble?"

"What's gotten into you, Lacey?"

"What's Lucas talking about, anyway?"

"Somebody pass the cream and sugar."

Lacey didn't hear any of it. Didn't see any of it. All she could see was the dread and anger in Gavin's infuriated gaze. He didn't trust her enough to even tell her goodbye. Maybe because he'd known she wouldn't let him go without her.

Well, now he was going to find out that

he could trust her, and her family, too. Because now he didn't have any other choice.

A couple of hours later it had all taken a turn for the worse. Her family now knew the whole story. And . . . they weren't taking it so well.

"Do you realize how dangerous this is?" Lorna asked Lacey as they walked with Willa through the wet gardens. The rain had stopped briefly, but the dark clouds to the west threatened to burst forth again at any time. They'd left Mick and Lucas talking with Gavin in the kitchen. Interrogating him, no doubt.

Lacey nodded, then stopped by an ancient crape myrtle. The vivid hot-pink blooms were gone, dried and mostly fallen away now that fall had come. "I know exactly how dangerous it is, but you have to understand. I believe in Gavin."

Lorna stared hard at her, as if trying to read her mind. "Why? Because he's handsome and intriguing? Because he's exotic and different? Because he's the first man you've even been remotely connected to since —"

Lacey pivoted, anger stifling her words. "Since Neil? Do you think I'm that desperate, that pathetic, Lorna? That I'd jump

228

at the chance to be with another man, any man? I've had plenty of opportunities before this, but you of all people know that my grief has held me prisoner. Look at Justin! He and I could easily have . . . we could have become close if I'd chosen to do so. But I didn't. I couldn't."

Willa had remained silent, watching the two sisters talk things out. Now she spoke up. "Speaking of Justin, he's been hovering around all morning, Lacey. He's asking questions, too."

"I know," Lacey said on a sigh. "He came by last night, but he didn't see Gavin. I wish I could explain things, but he doesn't need to get involved. I wish I could find Justin attractive and settle down with him, but it's just not that way between us. Oh, I do sound pathetic."

"No, you don't," Lorna said, taking Lacey's hand in hers. "And I don't think you're desperate, either. Justin has always been around. He's as dependable as the sun and the moon, and we've all taken him for granted. This man — Gavin — is different. And that's what worries me. Are you sure you aren't caught up in something you can't control — and I don't mean the political scandal and all the people who might be out to harm Gavin and you. I'm worried about that, of course, but I'm also worried about your emotional state. Don't let this man drag you down with him, Lacey."

Lacey looked at her sister. In spite of the concern in her eyes, Lorna was glowing with health and happiness, lush with joy. Lacey paled in comparison. It made her feel sick to her stomach to think her sister might be right. Was she rushing desperately and blindly into a relationship that would only lead to another heartbreak?

"I was doing just fine until y'all decided to come home and check up on me."

"Don't go getting defensive," Lorna retorted, one hand resting on her rounded stomach.

Willa ran a hand through the short blond hair that framed her oval face, causing her jade hoop earrings to sway against her long neck. "Lucas insisted on coming home once he heard about the town house being broken into. We love you, Lacey."

Lacey pulled her hand away from Lorna's, then went to sit on a lattice-backed bench near the butterfly garden. The old wood felt damp against the fabric of her skirt. "I know you're all concerned, which is why I tried to keep this from you to begin with, but I have to defend Gavin. You weren't there. You didn't see the pain and . . . despair in his eyes when he asked me to help him."

Lorna slowly eased down beside her. "No, we weren't there. But are you sure you didn't let that get to you? What if it's all an act? Now that we know who he really is, that we're harboring someone wanted in connection with some serious crimes, I just have to wonder if he hasn't been using you."

Lacey lowered her head to stare down at the maple leaves that had fallen on the path. "How could he be using me? Nothing has happened, except that I brought him here to keep those men from finding him. They would have killed him."

"And they could have killed you," Willa reminded her.

"Gavin protected me. We . . . we helped each other. He's been very polite, very concerned. That's why he was trying to leave this morning. He was trying to protect me, to keep me safe." She stopped, held a hand to her mouth. "I did lend him some money to buy the equipment."

"What equipment?" Lorna asked, her green eyes going wide. "How much money?"

"He needed a laptop and cell phone. He lost his other phone when his father's men were chasing us. And besides, we think they traced it. That's probably how they found us at the town house — he tried to call his mother once."

Lorna groaned. "Do you hear yourself? Being chased, having to replace expensive equipment, so Gavin can get the goods on his own father? What have you gotten yourself into?"

"Gavin will pay me back for the equipment," Lacey said. "I know he will. And after the things he's told me about his father, I think the man needs to be brought down a peg or two."

Lorna got up then, but Lacey didn't miss the worried look she shot Willa. "But what will Gavin do if he's behind bars and you get implicated for helping him? What if he's the guilty one, and not his father? Can he ever repay you if you lose your heart to him, plus go to jail for helping him?"

Confusion raged in Lacey's mind. But she kept remembering last night, and how Gavin had held her there underneath the old oak tree. She remembered his words. Even in Spanish, she'd understood what he was trying to tell her. Or had she just imagined that he'd offered her his heart?

Then she thought about the necklace he wore, the medallion he refused to remove from around his neck.

"I've already lost my heart to him," she told Lorna. "And I won't be going to jail. I trust Gavin and I intend to see this through until the end."

Lorna let out a frustrated groan. "No matter what that end might be?"

"Did you give up on Mick? Did you listen to everyone else? Did Lucas give up on Willa — no, he followed her to New York, held fast even though she told him to stay away."

Willa leaned against a trellis, folded her arms over her green silk sweater, a bittersweet smile on her face. "The Dorsettes are a stubborn lot."

"Well, everyone *else* wanted Mick and me to be together," Lorna reminded her. "This is different."

"Not so different," Lacey said as she got up to walk back to the house. Then she turned to stare at her sister and her new sister-in-law. "You — both of you — were in love and you were running from that love. Lorna, you didn't want to admit how you felt about Mick. And Willa, you were battling a serious illness. But you couldn't deny what you felt, either of you. I'm in love again, too . . . but I'm running *toward* that love. I've loved and lost before, so I've learned a thing or two. Every minute is precious. I'm not going to deny my feelings — not when my instincts tell me it's so right."

"She's got a point," Willa said, smiling softly again as she started walking with Lacey. "And every minute is precious. I should know that."

Lorna followed them back up the path, frowning. "Lacey, I don't want to deny you any happiness. You deserve that and more. But, honey, this is very dangerous."

"I'll be okay, I promise," Lacey told her. "Gavin knows what he's doing — he's very smart and capable."

"Oh, really? Then why is he hiding out here?"

"He had to have a quiet place to plan his strategy," Lacey replied. "You have to believe me, Lorna. Gavin is trying to clear his name."

Lorna stood there for a minute, then she hugged her sister close. "I wish Aunt Hilda were here."

"Me, too," Lacey said. "But we can't rely on her forever, you know."

"I know. So we're just going to have to turn it over to God. And I trust you to do what you think is right. Just be careful."

Lacey wiped a tear away, then smiled. "It probably doesn't matter now, anyway. Gavin was planning on leaving this morning when Lucas caught him. I don't think he really wants me around anymore, because he has this misguided sense of not being good enough for me, I think, but I haven't had a chance to find out how he really feels."

"I'm sure he cares about you. If he was leaving, it's for your own protection," Willa said. "And he is being smart regarding that. If he knows what he's doing, then let him go. You and he can find each other when this mess is cleared up and he's a free man. If that happens."

"It will."

"Then maybe you should listen to him and stop interfering."

"Hmmm. Maybe so. Or maybe he really is done with me and it's time for him to move on. Maybe I was wrong about him after all. I just don't know. I thought I knew, but now I'm beginning to wonder." She looked toward the house where they'd left the men. "Either way, I'm going to find him and talk about it until we reach an agreement."

"Well, Prescott, you and I agree on one

thing at least," Lucas told Gavin as they stood on the boat dock near the bayou. "You need to move on. You've put Lacey and this family in a very dangerous position."

"*Si,*" Gavin said, his gaze moving out over the brackish swamp waters. "I've been trying to tell you that all day."

Mick stood with them, his thumbs hooked in the belt loops of his jeans. "Lacey has a good heart, Gavin. She . . . she wouldn't know how to turn away from someone who's hurt or in need."

"I saw that in her right away," Gavin said, hating the way his voice grew raspy and weak. "I don't want to hurt your sister, Lucas."

Lucas still looked doubtful. "Man, if these people are as nasty as you say, what's to keep them from coming after Lacey even after you leave?"

"After tonight, it should all be over," Gavin told him. "I'm going back there to find what I need — to clear my name and to put the senator away for good."

"And if that doesn't happen?" Mick asked, his gaze direct and unflinching.

"If . . . if something goes wrong," Gavin said, stopping to find the right words, "then Lacey will be safe. They will come after *me*. They don't know anything about her."

"They broke in to her hotel room and her house," Lucas reminded him. "And they shot at both of you."

"I don't think they found anything to trace back here," Gavin replied. "Lacey and I were very careful, and I've been careful in not giving her any details other than what she'd hear on the news anyway."

"Yeah, right. That's why you got stabbed and shot at, *hein?*" Lucas scowled at him, his dark eyes wary. "We're not that far from New Orleans. They could have followed y'all."

"We made sure they didn't."

Mick had been quiet, but now he looked up. "So you hid out here, ordered some sort of hotshot equipment so you can go back to your father's fancy costume party and hack into his computer system to find the dirt on him?"

"That's about the gist of it," Gavin said. "And I will pay Lacey back, for everything."

"I know that for true," Lucas retorted. "I'm going to personally see to it."

Gavin felt weary from the day's events. They'd managed to keep him away from Lacey, which was probably a good thing, because in his state of mind he just might kidnap her and take her with him, just to make her see reason. But he still had to get to New Orleans by nightfall — without Lacey.

He looked at Lucas and gave it one more shot. "Listen, I don't have much left except my honor. And I will honor Lacey. I couldn't do that to her. She's a good woman." He went still and quiet as he stared down into the bayou. He remembered holding her close while she cried. He remembered kissing her, and wishing he was worthy of her love. "And the strangest part — she somehow sees the good in me, if there's any left."

Lucas pushed at his shoulder. "*Bonté*, you're in love with Lacey!"

Mick lifted his dark brows in surprise, then glanced at Gavin. "Oh, man. That does complicate matters."

Gavin nodded, then expelled a slow breath. "It's all complicated. And *sí*, I do love her." He could admit that now, now that he'd been forced to lay all his cards on the table. Saying it out loud only added to his woes, however. "But . . . you can't tell her that."

Lucas's expression changed from wariness to understanding. "So you really were trying to leave to protect her."

Again Gavin nodded. "And now that you're all here, I can leave knowing she's going to be all right."

"And then what?" Lucas asked. "What happens when this is all over?"

Gavin grabbed Lucas's shirtfront, bunching the soft cotton in his fingers. "I'm coming back for her, whether you like it or not."

Lucas actually chuckled. "I get you, *mon ami*. For true, if you love her and can make her a good life and you get your name cleared and all criminal activity put aside — you know, little things like that tend to cloud a relationship — then you have my blessings. But that remains to be seen, *oui?*"

Gavin let go, then breathed a sigh of relief. "Then can I please leave now?"

"But what about Lacey?" Mick asked. "She's of the mind that she's going with you."

Gavin started toward the garage. "You'll just have to change her mind."

"You know Lacey," Lucas replied. "That won't be easy."

"Keep her here," Gavin said, unable to say anything more. "Keep her safe."

Mick and Lucas watched as he headed

down the path. Then he turned. "Oh, by the way, Lacey said I could use the SUV."

Lucas frowned, then shrugged. "But of course. I guess you'll send a new one if anything happens, right?"

"Right," Gavin called. Then he stopped to wave to them. *"Gracias."*

Lucas turned back to Mick. "He can thank us when he gets this mess straightened out."

"And when he comes back for Lacey," Mick said.

"If he comes back," Lucas said, glancing over his shoulder as he heard the SUV start up. "If."

Chapter Fourteen

He almost made it out of the garage. But then Gavin spotted them. Two men in a dark sedan, parked just outside the electronic gate. He could see them through the trees and shrubbery, all of which were just bare enough that he had a straight line of vision from the secluded garage to the main road. Thankfully, the gate was shut and they couldn't get in without the entry code. But why were they parked there?

FBI? he wondered. Or maybe someone posing as FBI.

Gavin quickly parked the SUV back in the garage, then skirted the back wall and made his way back up the bayou toward the mansion. He darted here and there, hoping to make it back inside the house to warn Lacey and the others.

He was just coming around the summerhouse when Justin Hayes stepped out of the bushes.

"Who are you?"

Gavin sighed long and hard, not wanting yet another fight on his hands. "I'm a friend of Lacey's. I forgot something up at the house."

Justin squinted at him, then frowned. "I don't recall you being up at the house."

"I was," Gavin told him, glancing over his shoulder. "Lacey was kind enough to let me hang out here for a couple of days."

"With her?"

Gavin nodded, then started up the path.

"She didn't tell me that last night when I saw her."

Gavin shrugged, tried to act nonchalant. "It was late and she probably saw no reason to tell you."

"Is this what all the fuss is about?" Justin asked, following Gavin toward the back of the house.

"What fuss?" Gavin wanted to slug the inquisitive man, but held his temper. It had been a long day and it was probably going to get worse before it got better.

"I've seen everyone huddled together," Justin said, coming around to stop in front of Gavin. "Lacey seems upset. Is that because of you?"

Forced to face the man, Gavin gave the scrawny redheaded garden warrior a long, hard look. "Lacey has a lot on her mind. Now, I really need to get back to the house."

"I'll go with you, then."

Gavin threw up his hands. "Fine. That's fine."

He and Justin were greeted at the door by Lucas and Mick.

"Back so soon?" Lucas asked, a wry smirk on his face.

"We've got problems," Gavin said on a low whisper, thumbing over his shoulder toward the road. "It's either the feds or some of my father's henchmen. Either way, I can't get past them. Any ideas?"

"I've got lots of ideas," Lucas replied, the smirk gone as he went into full alert. "But you probably wouldn't like any of them."

Justin trailed behind Gavin, but he hadn't heard the conversation. "Why is he lurking around the gardens, Lucas? Is he really a friend of Lacey's?"

"Good questions, Justin," Lucas said, slapping Justin on the back. "And the answers are 'I don't know' and 'Yes, we think so.'"

"Do you need me to escort him off the property?"

Gavin whirled to glare at Justin. "Just try it, *amigo.* I suggest you go back to your potting soil."

"I don't like your tone, mister," Justin

243

said, his hands on his hips, his freckled face turning red.

"Justin!" Lacey came into the hallway, her gaze sweeping over her brother and Gavin. "Justin, this is . . . my friend Gavin. It's okay, really. Gavin and I need to have a private talk." She turned to face Gavin, the look in her eyes accusing. "I've been looking for you."

"I don't like this, Lacey," Justin said. "Was he here last night?"

"Yes." She nodded. "He was in his room asleep."

Justin took that in, frowned, then whirled toward the door. "You could have told me."

"I'm sorry," Lacey said, her eyes still on Gavin.

Justin just waved a hand and kept walking. "I'll be in the front gardens if y'all need me." Then he shot a glance at Lacey over his shoulder. "Which I doubt you will."

"You hurt his feelings," Lucas pointed out.

"I've made a mess of everything," Lacey said, taking Gavin by the arm. "But I'm about to straighten it all out."

"Hold on." Gavin pulled his arm away. "Lacey, we've got more visitors. And I don't think these two are related to you."

Lucas stepped between them. "Your friend here is bringing all sorts of folks out to the country — bad folks."

Lacey's eyes widened. "Lucas, you've got to get us out of here."

"Excuse me?"

"You can take us through the swamp. We can get a car in the village so we can get to New Orleans."

Lucas threw up his hands in frustration. "Well, why not just get the Piper and fly right out of here?"

"That would be even better," Lacey said, completely serious.

"You have gone off your rocker," Lucas told her. "Lacey, there are men out there, watching the house."

Gavin ran a hand over his hair. "I just need to get out of here before they find me. They probably want to ask some questions, get some information. But we can't be sure. If they get to me, I'll never make it to New Orleans tonight."

Mick backed into the hallway from the front parlor. "One of the men came in through the gate at the end of the oaks. Just walked right in. We need to check that lock. I just saw him talking to Justin."

Gavin watched as Lacey's skin went pale.

"Justin will tell them everything, Lucas. He'll tell them Gavin is here."

"She's right," Mick said, glancing back over his shoulder to the yard. "Where are Lorna and Willa?"

"They're upstairs, unpacking," Lacey said. "Mick, go up and tell them to stay there."

Mick hurried up the long central hallway to the winding staircase, then shouted down as he looked through the French windows. "Justin is walking with him toward the house."

"And what about you?" Gavin asked. "Lacey, this is why I tried to leave. Now I've put you and your family in even more danger."

"You got that right, buddy," Lucas retorted, his eyes watchful. "Why didn't you just keep going while you had the chance?"

"Because those goons were out there waiting," Gavin said, fully aware that Lacey was staring at him with a hurt expression. "I didn't want to leave without warning you. And I didn't want them to break in to the house."

"Well, one of 'em got in somehow," Lucas said. He turned to stare out the glass-paned double doors. "And Justin is bringing him inside."

Lacey glanced around. "He'll see us." Then she grabbed Gavin by the hand. "Come with me."

Lucas watched her, his hands on his hips. "Where are you going?"

"The elevator," she whispered. "We can take it to the second floor and hide up there until you get rid of him."

"*Moi?*" Lucas pointed to his chest. "*I'm* supposed to get rid of them?"

"Lucas," she said, pleading, "just do this for me."

"Oh, and then I get to somehow transport both of you through the swamp to the other side of the village, right?"

"You are a very good brother," Lacey replied as she dragged Gavin with her.

Gavin didn't hear all of Lucas's reply, but the part he did hear didn't sound encouraging. He stopped, lifted Lacey's hand away from his arm. "I'm going out there to face them. I can't do this, Lacey."

"Hush," she said, all business now. "Just come with me until we find out who they are, at least."

He couldn't argue with that logic, so he followed her.

"What's this?" he asked while she pressed a discreet brass button beside what looked like a door underneath the curve of the staircase.

"It's a small elevator my aunt uses to get upstairs. She has a very bad arthritic knee and has to use a cane."

Gavin watched as the small white door swished open. The elevator looked like a closet door tucked behind the stairwell. "Very smart," he said as he entered with Lacey.

She closed the door, then turned and bumped into him. He couldn't resist. He took her into his arms and kissed her. "I'm sorry."

She looked up at him with confusion and longing. "For getting me in this mess, or for leaving me to clean up after you? Or maybe for planning on leaving me, period?"

He touched a hand to her cheek. "You're hurt and angry. I don't blame you."

"Let me go," she whispered, her gaze falling away.

"I can't. It's a very small elevator."

"It's made for one person."

"Then stand close to me."

She tried to squirm away, to turn her head.

He pulled her back, kissed her again. "I'll miss your scent, Lacey. You smell like a garden at midnight."

"Don't." She pushed at his chest with her hands. "Don't do that to me. You . . . you were just going to leave — you were on your way again when you saw those men, weren't you?"

"Yes," he admitted. "I don't want you in New Orleans tonight. It's too dangerous."

"But I thought we were a team. I thought we were in this together."

Gavin touched his forehead to hers. She was warm and soft and so sweet. "Lacey, we can't be in this together. This is my problem. I have to straighten this out alone."

"Without me?"

"*Sí*, but not because I don't want you with me."

"Maybe because you don't want me at all."

"I do, *querida*. I do."

The doors of the elevator creaked open as he finished his declaration. "I want us to be together, Lacey. But after this is over."

Gavin turned to find Lorna and Willa standing at an upstairs window, a knowing look on their feminine faces.

He supposed they'd heard that last statement.

And he really didn't care.

Lacey shot out of the elevator, her face flushed. "Where's Lucas?"

Lorna put a finger to her lips. "He's down there giving a good ol' Cajun run-around to our visitor. Mick is with him, just to make sure the stranger doesn't stray up here."

Willa nodded. "And Justin is backing him up."

"Justin?"

"Yes. He brought the man inside, introduced him as Special Agent Dan Gleason from the FBI, then proceeded to tell the man that no one here knows anything about any investigation of any state senator. I think he's trying to talk the man into a tizzy so he'll just leave. Right now they're all discussing crop rotation, or something."

Gavin saw the look of surprise and appreciation on Lacey's face. Maybe she had feelings for Justin after all. Maybe she regretted putting Justin in such a position.

"Y'all could hide in there," Lorna suggested, pointing toward a small sitting room between the bedrooms. "If you want to finish your . . . elevator conversation."

"We're through talking," Lacey said as she whirled past them into the room.

"Oh, okay." Lorna gave Gavin a penetrating look, but let him pass.

He went into the whitewashed room and closed the door to the overly interested women in the hallway. "We are not finished."

Lacey stood at a small alcove window, surrounded by antique white wicker furniture and floral curtains, staring down at the gardens. "I think we are. You're going to walk away and I'll never see you again."

Anger and agitation made his words harsh. "Have you stopped to think that I have a lot riding on tonight? Have you considered that I might not be *able* to ever see you again?"

She whirled, her blue eyes like shattered ice. "I've considered it all, Gavin. I've prayed for you. For your safety, for your integrity. I've asked God to give you the strength to get through this. I know this is a dangerous thing. I know this is for keeps. That's why —" She stopped, took a long breath. "That's why I want to be there with you. I just feel that if I'm there I can somehow protect you, keep you from harm. Isn't that silly?"

Gavin came across the soft woven rug to tug her around. "You *are* my angel. That's why *I* have to *protect* you."

"Why does everyone treat me as if I

might break?" she asked, her eyes wide and misty. "I've had to be so strong, Gavin. *All my life*. I lived in a jungle as a child. I watched my parents talk to people about God, watched them bring so many people to Christ. Then I watched them being brutally murdered. I came here, to this safe retreat, and I found love with a man who was so wonderful, so good, so strong. After we got married I thought I had it all, and then everything good and pure was taken from me. A person can't go through those tragedies without some sort of strength. And yet everyone seems to think I'm so fragile. I won't break. I haven't broken yet."

He stood there, watching her face, seeing the grief and pain in her eyes, and then he asked, "But what if I'm the one who does finally break you?"

She turned away, back toward the window. "Then . . . I'll remember our time together and I'll go back to my life here. I'll stay strong in my faith. That's all I can do."

He knew she was being brave. He knew she would mourn yet again. And this time she might not ever come out of her retreat.

Which was why he had to get away. Without her.

So he tried to make her understand.

"Lacey, these past few days with you have been like . . . like coming home. You are such an example of the kind of life I have longed for, the kind of life I might have had if my real father hadn't died." He leaned close to whisper in her ear. "I want to spend time with you. I want to take you to Spain and show you the home of my ancestors. I want to walk through these gardens with you, day and night. I want . . . so much."

She turned then, falling against him, her arms going around his neck. "Gavin, you do care. I was afraid —"

He hushed her with another kiss. "I would never hurt you. That much I can promise."

She bobbed her head, touched a hand to his hair. "And I only want to help you. I told you I believe in you. Why can't you believe in me?"

He reached up, his hands holding her face. "I do believe in you, and because of you, I'm beginning to believe in myself again. And . . . I'm beginning to trust in God again. You have given me that gift."

"I want to give you more," she said, her eyes filling with tears. "Gavin, I'm so afraid if you leave, I won't ever see you again. And there's still so much I need to know, so many questions."

He kissed her again. Then he lifted his head and said, "I promise you, I will be back. I will come back here for you, no matter what."

"How can I be sure?"

Gavin stepped back, then pulled the silver-chained cross necklace from around his neck. He placed it over Lacey's head, then held his hand there on it as it lay cradled against the soft cashmere of her sweater, its intricately threaded strands tangling with her pearls. "I want you to keep this with you until you see me again. If . . . if something happens to me, this will give you the answers you seek."

Lacey touched her hand over his, her eyes bright with tears. "I can't take this, Gavin. You need it with you. You told me to never take it away from you."

"You didn't take it," he said as he brought her hand up to his lips. "I'm *giving* it to you. I want you to have it."

"But —"

"I know now that I have Christ to protect me. You taught me that."

He held her there, watching the tears stream down her face. "Keep this close, Lacey. Remember it will help you through whatever comes next."

She nodded, her voice husky and soft. "And you'll come back to me, right?"

"I promise, *bella*. I promise." He turned to leave.

"Where are you going now? What are you going to do?"

"I'm going to go down there and tell that agent everything I know and hope he's really with the FBI and he believes me. Then I'm going to New Orleans to confront my parents. I'm tired of running."

"So here's the deal," Lucas said an hour later as they all sat around the kitchen, their sandwiches mostly untouched. "Gavin is headed to New Orleans."

The rain had returned with a vengeance and the weatherman had predicted the storm brewing along the coast could become a full-blown hurricane by nightfall.

"We feel certain that our friend Gleason was really with the FBI. Gavin confronted the man and pretty much made him call everybody from the governor on up to prove that. And now the FBI has agreed to let Gavin wear a wire when he goes to the ball tonight, in exchange for complete immunity. Gavin will dress in costume, only he'll be packing a little transmitter that will feed any conversations he has right back to our friend Gleason and his sidekick in the sedan or the van or whatever they decide to hide in outside the mansion gates. And of course while Gavin is there, he's planning his side operation of tapping in to his father's secret files, too. What a party animal."

He'd said that last to lighten things up, but Lacey couldn't find the energy to smile. It just wasn't funny. She sat with her hands wrapped around a coffee mug. She was still numb, still worried. So worried. "They're sending Gavin in there as a decoy. They're testing him to see if he's loyal to the government or his father. How can he deal with that? How?"

Lucas cast a glance at Lorna, then touched a hand to Lacey's arm. "Gavin knows what he's doing — you said that yourself. He was up front with Agent Gleason, told the man exactly what had happened. And he made it seem as if he'd forced you to hide him here, and we naturally backed him up on that one, so you're in the clear for now."

"How comforting," Lacey replied, the roar of rain only echoing the roar of fear and rage inside her head and heart. "I should be there, too. I could do something, anything, to help Gavin."

"He didn't want you there," Lorna reminded her. "Why don't you go on up to your room and try to rest."

Lacey got up to stare down at her brother and sister. "I don't want to rest. I don't want to be pampered and protected. Don't you understand? Gavin turned himself in to protect me."

"And to clear his name," Mick reminded her from his position by the counter. "Lacey, the man seems like a decent fellow. He did the only thing he could do. He stopped running. And this way, he gets to do what he'd set out to do, but with the backing of the FBI."

"What if he's walking into a trap?" Lacey asked, looking from one anxious face to another.

She clutched the heavy silver jeweled cross in her hand, praying with all her might that Gavin would be safe. *Just keep him safe, Lord. Keep him safe and I'll accept whatever happens after that.*

Willa got up to come and put her arm around Lacey. "I think Lucas is right. I think Gavin knows exactly what he's doing. He really grilled that FBI agent today, asking just as many questions of him as that man did of Gavin. He made it very clear that he knew his rights, he knew what to expect and he knew he had an edge."

"He is a lawyer," Lucas reminded her with a cynical smile.

Lacey looked up then. "What edge?"

"Gavin told the man he already had part of the encrypted code to his father's secret files," Lucas said. "He made a deal with Gleason, said he'd give over the files after tonight. After he had a chance to go back in and find the missing links."

Lacey stared at Willa, then turned to face Lucas. "So you think Gleason is banking on that information, just in case Gavin fails tonight?"

"That's what we believe," Mick told her. "We all talked about it after they left. But I think Gavin has a plan that he didn't share with our friend from the FBI."

"Which means your new boyfriend is very smart," Lucas told her, a grin on his face. "So cheer up, *chère*. It's gonna all turn out okay. I promise."

Remembering Gavin's promise, Lacey held tightly to the blue topaz centered in the necklace.

Willa looked down at the cross. "That's a beautiful necklace. I saw it on Gavin before."

"He gave it to me," Lacey said. "As a promise that he'd be back."

"Then there you have it," Lucas said, coming around the table to put his hands on her shoulders. "Now, I suggest we all hunker down and wait out this storm. I'm going to go out and find Justin. He was checking to make sure everything was secure in the gardens and outbuildings."

"I'll help, too," Mick replied. "We need to get it all done before nightfall."

Lacey watched them put on raincoats and galoshes and head out the back door. "Another storm."

Lorna got up to put their dishes in the sink. "Let's hope this one doesn't bring more flooding or damage."

Willa stifled a yawn. "I'm sorry. I'm going to go on up. I'm so tired from taking that early flight."

"Of course," Lorna told her. "You need to rest anyway." Then she touched Willa's slender arm. "We're so glad you're home and that you're healing. I'm sure Dr. Savoy will give you a clean bill of health next week, too."

"Thanks," Willa replied. "As much as I enjoyed our honeymoon, I have to admit it's good to be back home."

"She's bouncing back from all the radiation and chemo," Lorna said after Willa had left. "She looks great and I like the short hairstyle."

Lacey nodded. "I'm thankful that her cancer is in remission. Lucas loves her so much." For a while she moved about the kitchen in silence. Then she turned to face her sister. "I'm going, Lorna."

"Going where?"

"New Orleans. I'm going to go to the senator's mansion to find Gavin."

"You can't do that," Lorna said, shaking her head. "Haven't you heard a word we said here?"

"I heard it all, and I'm going. Gavin might have a Plan B, but I want to be there to see it with my own eyes."

"So you're going to go out in a raging thunderstorm, then head right into the path of a possible hurricane?"

"Yes. And I need you to help me. I have to come up with another costume, so Gavin won't spot me too soon."

"Oh, no." Lorna paced back and forth, her hands on her rounded stomach. "I won't do it. For one thing, Lucas would have a fit. And Gavin — we promised him we'd keep you here."

"You don't have to honor that. I'll explain to him that it was my decision."

"Lacey, I don't like this —"

"Well, we didn't like it when Lucas took the Piper and flew to New York to find Willa, either, did we? But that didn't stop *him*. And I didn't like it the day you decided to stay here during the flood, but that didn't stop *you*. I'm going and that's that."

The door opened then and Justin walked in, dripping water from his yellow rain slicker. He looked up to find Lorna and Lacey locked in a battle of wills. "What's going on?"

"Justin," Lacey said, moving across the kitchen to him, "I need your help."

"Sure. What is it?"

"Can you bring your truck up to the house for me in about half an hour? I have to go out."

"In this weather? Lacey, it's bad out there."

"Justin, I really need you to do this."

Lorna groaned and threw up her hands. "Don't listen to her, Justin."

But Justin was listening, thankfully. He stood there wet and dejected, his eyes on Lacey. "You want to find *him*, don't you?"

"I have to, Justin. I have to get to New Orleans before this storm gets any worse."

"And you want me to help you?"

"Yes. I just need you to bring the truck around."

Justin stood there, then nodded. "I'm going with you."

"What? No, you don't have to do that."

"Lacey, if you're determined to find this man, then I'm going with you, just in case you need me."

Lorna gave Lacey a warning look. "Justin, that's way too . . . dangerous."

"I know," Justin replied, his steady gaze on Lacey. "And I also know that Lacey will never have feelings for me the way I have for her. So . . . if she really cares about this other man and wants to find him, then I'll help her out." He smiled at Lacey, a sad resolved smile. "I just want you to be happy again."

"Oh, Justin," Lacey said as she rushed to hug him tight. "You are a good friend. I wish —"

He hushed her with a hand on her mouth. "Don't wish for things you don't really want. Go get ready. I'll bring the truck around."

He left, still dripping.

"I can't believe you're doing this," Lorna said. "And you know I can't go with you."

"No, you need to stay here and take care of that baby. But you can call our friend Sheila and ask her to have a costume ready

262

for me when I arrive in New Orleans. Tell her I'll pay extra for making her come out to her shop in a storm."

"Lucas is going to be so angry."

"Lucas has been impulsive and head-strong all of his life. I've watched him do things his way for a very long time. Now it's my turn."

"Aunt Hilda would disapprove."

"Yes, but she'd also understand. All my life I've tried to be the strong one. It was just a front, and you all saw right through it. Why else would you rush home and become so overly protective? As long as I stayed quiet and dependable, you thought I was safe. But now I need to do this, Lorna. I need to break out of that facade I've created."

"Did you have to choose such a risky way to do it?"

"I don't have a choice. Gavin needs me."

Lorna finally nodded, sighed in defeat, then hugged Lacey close. "Don't do anything stupid."

"I love him, Lorna."

"I know, I know. I just wish loving him wasn't so dangerous."

"Say a prayer for us, then."

"I will. And please, call me so I won't worry."

"All right." Lacey hugged her sister, grabbed a raincoat off the coatrack in the office, then ran to get into the waiting truck.

The day turned into night and the rain picked up, slashing and bashing the house and gardens.

Just one more storm to get through, Lacey thought. Then it would all be over, one way or another. She held her hand to Gavin's cross and prayed.

And remembered his promise.

Chapter Fifteen

In spite of the threat of a hurricane, the Prescott mansion was open for business. Gavin had managed to slip in with another group of revelers who'd instructed their limo driver to pull up underneath the round portico at the front door to avoid the driving rain. He was in heavy disguise, dressed as a cross between Mozart and George Washington in a resplendent gold brocade waistcoat and pale cream breeches, with a white wig and an elaborate golden mask that covered most of his face.

And he was wired to the teeth. He didn't like it, but since he'd involved Lacey and her family, he was willing to compromise with the FBI to prove she had nothing to do with this. It was a one-man show now.

But what Agent Gleason didn't know wouldn't hurt him and just might help Gavin, too. His friend Harry Crane was waiting in the wings in a seedy motel room in the Quarter, with all the equipment they needed hooked up and online. He hadn't even told Lacey about Harry's willingness to help him out. That was Plan B.

Now Gavin merged and mingled with some of New Orleans' finest, noting with relief that no one seemed to recognize him. Whenever anyone inquired, he only nodded in greeting and stayed silent. These people wore masks, too, but Gavin knew even without a masque ball to hide their identities, they all had their share of secrets.

Outside, the rain hissed and howled, forcing his mother to keep shut the eight exquisite ceiling-to-floor glass-paned doors that took up one huge rounded wall leading to the terrace. That meant that everyone had to stay inside away from the sloping shores leading down to Lake Pontchartrain, making the mansion even more crowded than usual and the whole scene chaotic and confusing — something that worked along with the music and merriment in Gavin's favor.

He stood in a corner now, nursing a crystal goblet of mineral water, while he watched the senator and his mother play host across the wide hallway in another room. The senator was dressed fittingly as the pirate Lafitte. And his beautiful, deceiving mother was dressed as Marie Antoinette.

In spite of their sequined masks, Gavin

knew his parents. They commanded attention and respect as they held court in a long receiving line. He could hear their laughter, see the sparkle in their eyes. But he also saw how they stood alert, their eyes searching when no one else was looking or passing. It made him sick to his stomach all over again.

After a discreet time, Gavin made his way toward the long hallway, heading in the direction of his father's office at the back of the first floor. He had to get to the computer, find what he needed and get out. Then if he had the opportunity, he was supposed to confront his father, face-to-face, or in this case, he thought wryly, mask-to-mask. Agent Gleason was depending on that little encounter.

Gavin hated having to force his own mother and father to come clean, hated wearing a wire so he could get information from them. He just plain hated all of it. He thought of Bayou le Jardin and his time there with Lacey, thought of how she'd made him feel — whole and worthy and worth fighting for. She was a spark of goodness and light in a dark, ugly world. His world.

He wanted to find that goodness and light again in her arms. He wanted to go back to her world. So he went about his work with a grim determination.

About thirty minutes into the party, Gavin strolled into the long formal dining room, where the massive buffet kept several caterers running back and forth to the kitchen. He was rounding a set of open double doors when he looked up and into the eyes of a beautiful woman dressed in red and black as a Spanish flamenco dancer.

A blue-eyed flamenco dancer who smelled like a garden at midnight. And wore pearls.

Gavin blinked, thought he was imagining things.

Then she reached out a hand to him. "Dance with me, Mozart?"

"Lacey?"

She nodded, just a slight tilt of her head.

He tugged her close, then whirled her around to the wall, making sure no one was watching them. "What are you doing here?"

"I always see things through, Gavin. You should know that about me. Even if it requires wearing a fake beauty mark and a terribly ruffled red satin ball gown."

He stared down at her, saw the determination in her eyes through the slits of her black silk domino. "Where did you get the costume?"

She leaned close, her black curling wig touching on his shoulder, her lace-edged fan shielding their faces. "At a friend's shop in the Quarter. She sells costumes for Mardi Gras. I had to come up with something different. This is Lorna's idea of getting your attention, I suppose. She called ahead and ordered it for me."

He urged her closer, then said into her ear, "You aren't supposed to be here, *señorita.*" But he was sure glad to have her in his arms again.

"And you aren't supposed to be under suspicion for racketeering and extortion, but you are."

"Lacey," he whispered, awe in the one word. "Lacey."

"Just hold me," she told him. "Dance with me until we can sneak out of here. I'll stand watch for you. I'll distract anyone who comes in. I'll do whatever is needed. Please don't send me away."

Gavin sighed long and hard. "The FBI is listening to us, Lacey. Our friend Gleason won't like you interfering."

She leaned close, her eyes on Gavin while she talked. "Agent Gleason, please stay back and trust me. I know what Gavin is planning and I won't jeopardize anything." Then she smiled up at Gavin. "There, that should take care of him."

Gavin knew that wherever Gleason was, he was probably moaning in outrage right now. But Lacey was here, and there was nothing to be done about it. "How'd you get here?"

"Justin drove me."

"Justin?"

She stilled him with a finger to his lips. "Justin thinks I'm in love with you."

Gavin's heart stopped. He didn't know whether she was flirting, or whether she truly believed that. He only knew that she'd make a remarkable spy. He couldn't read her at all.

So he just went with it. "I see. So because of that, he offered to get you here tonight, out of the goodness of his heart?"

She nodded. "Because he wants me to be happy, he agreed to help me find you."

"We'll get back to this later," he told her as they waltzed right out of the crowded doorway and into the hall. Then he stood back to look down at her. "Right now we have work to do."

"Let's go," she replied with a soft determination.

★ ★ ★

The office was electronically locked, of course, but Gavin tried the combination code he already knew, praying that it hadn't been changed. When the door clicked open, he breathed a sigh of relief, then tugged Lacey inside the room.

"This shouldn't take long," he whispered. "Just stand by the door and tell me if you hear or see anyone coming."

"Okay." She adjusted the tight bodice of her dress, then leaned close to the wall. Gavin noticed that she was wearing his medallion. She'd had it hidden before, but now she was clutching it in one hand as she waited. That brought him some comfort.

Still amazed that she'd managed to get here in this weather, and with her whole family warning her to stay put, he sat down at the computer and inserted a blank compact disk into the disk drive. Then he started keying in the codes he'd memorized and hidden away, hoping to gain access to the rest of the files. After a few minutes of file names racing by, he banged a hand on the desk. "I know it's here somewhere."

"Can't find what you need?" Lacey said in a loud whisper.

"No. There's a missing file — the money trail. It should show all the bank accounts — if there are any — that match up with the ones I've already traced, or at least it should show everything they've been paid, their hidden assets." He said this for the benefit of Agent Gleason, just in case the man got any notions of storming the palace too quickly.

"That sounds harder to figure out than my secret salad dressing recipe," Lacey said, nerves making her words echo strangely in the silent room.

"Well, right now I could use some secret recipes," Gavin replied on a low whisper. Then he stopped and went still. "Secret recipes."

Lacey stepped away from the door. "What is it, Gavin?"

"Secret recipes." He hit the computer keys with his fingers, quickly doing a file search. "My mother is notorious for getting secret recipes from the best chefs in town. They give them to her in exchange for her endorsements. One word from Nita Prescott can make or break a restaurant in this area. She has a computer file full of recipes she passes on to the cook."

"That's nice, but what does that have to do with your father's illegal money?"

Gavin watched the screen light up, saw the numbers there, then turned to Lacey. "It has everything to do with it. My mother is his private accountant. I just found the files, Lacey."

"Under secret recipes." It was a statement, a hushed statement of disbelief. "Your mother has all of this hidden in her . . . kitchen file?"

"*Sí,* she's labeled it *Recetas Familiares.* The family recipes."

Gavin turned away from the computer, waiting while the file downloaded onto the CD. In a matter of minutes he'd also transferred the information via e-mail to the encrypted files he'd already stored, which good ol' Harry should be receiving any minute now back at the hotel. Then Gavin dialed Harry's number on his cell phone to confirm that the information had been received. When he heard a distinctive beep at the end of the line, he knew Harry had stored the information in a secure spot. And he also knew that Agent Gleason would have a hard time trying to figure out what that beeping sound had been. Just Harry's way of letting Gavin know everything had gone as planned. The files were safe and even Agent Gleason would go crazy trying to crack them unless he had

Gavin alive and well and by his side. One more bit of insurance and extra protection his friend Harry had told him about. A good thing, since he'd been forced to leave most of his gadgets at Bayou le Jardin.

I'll have to take him to Antoine's for dinner when this is all over, Gavin silently promised.

Gavin turned around then. "We did it, Lacey. I've hidden the files until I can get to my laptop and download them again. And in a few minutes, I'll have a backup disk right here, too." He pointed toward the deep pocket of his brocade jacket. "This combined with the file codes I've already seen will prove they were hiding a substantial cash flow. And based on the language in these documents, I think I know where they've hidden it."

"Good, then we can get out of here." Lacey had been watching Gavin so closely, she didn't hear the footsteps in the hallway until it was almost too late.

But Gavin saw a shadow through the inch of open door. He held a finger to his lips, then motioned for Lacey to be quiet. Just another minute and the file would be finished, then he'd be home free. But Lacey apparently had other plans.

"Finish it," she whispered. "I'll stall whoever it is."

Before Gavin could make a move, she opened the door and smiled up at the big man who'd been about to enter the room, then carefully pulled the door shut with one hand, leaving it slightly open for Gavin's benefit.

"Well, hello there. I'm so sorry. I was looking for the powder room and . . . well, I seem to be lost."

"How'd you get in there?" Gavin heard the man ask. Great. That sounded like his old friend Randall. Not good.

"The door, silly," Lacey replied, sounding as calm as a belle at a barbecue. "I just opened it and went in."

"That door's supposed to be locked."

"Well, it isn't. Might want to do something about that. Now, where is the . . . uh —"

"Bathroom's down the hall, lady, to the left."

Gavin held his breath, waiting for the big man to leave. Then he heard him ask, "What are you waiting for?"

Lacey laughed again. "You're blocking my way."

"You need to leave," the man said, "so I can check this room and set the code on this door."

Gavin felt sweat trickling down between his shoulder blades. What was Lacey doing out there?

Then he heard her. "Can I ask you something?"

The man sighed. "What?"

"What kind of room is this anyway — I mean, is this the senator's office? I'm just fascinated with politics."

In spite of the tense situation, Gavin had to smile. Lacey was playing a Southern belle, dressed as a flamenco dancer. The woman had spunk, he'd give her that. But she was being too brave. Much too brave.

Gavin finished downloading the file, pulled the disk out and shut off the computer just as the door burst open.

He lost his breath as he saw Lacey being hauled back into the room, with Randall holding a gun to her head.

"I thought there was something fishy going on here," Randall said. "You two are in serious trouble."

Gavin gave Lacey a warning look as he stood holding his hands up in the air. At least they were both still masked. That would give them a fighting chance. Disguising his accent, he said, "Listen, we just wanted to be alone — you understand. We sorta stumbled in here."

"Guests aren't allowed in here," the man said. Then he spoke into an earpiece. "I found some intruders in the senator's office." He pushed Lacey toward Gavin, held the gun on them, then closed the door. "You two just sit tight."

Gavin immediately shielded Lacey with his body, then tried to reason with the man. Now would be a good time for Gleason to make his move, too. "Look, we were just trying to find some privacy." He grinned, inclined his head toward Lacey. "The *señorita* is shy."

"I'll just reckon," the big goon said, his leering gaze moving over Lacey. "That's sweet, but I have to keep you right here until the senator decides what to do with you."

Gavin let that soak in, wondering if Agent Gleason would beat his father to the punch, or just wait it out so he could get the confrontation he'd been promised. Gavin pretended to be bored with the whole thing. "We meant no harm. Just needed to slip away."

"This door is always locked," the man replied. "I'd call that breaking and entering."

"We walked right in," Lacey said, but Gavin shot her a warning look.

Soon the door burst open and the senator entered, followed by two dark-suited men. "What's going on, Randall?"

"I found these two — claim they wanted to be alone."

"I see." Senator Prescott took off his mask and pirate wig, then smiled. "You are guests in my home, but I can't tell who you are with those masks. Please remove them."

Lacey watched Gavin for her cue. If she'd only been able to stall that giant a little longer, they might be long gone by now. This was her fault.

Gavin held her close behind him, then turned to whisper, "Whatever happens, don't lose the necklace."

"Okay," she said, wondering what he had in mind.

Then Gavin turned to face his father. Lacey watched Senator Prescott's tanned face as Gavin peeled off his wig and mask. Recognition caused the senator to go pale.

He let out a hiss of breath. "Gavin. I should have known."

"*Gavino,*" Gavin said, the one word low and full of anger.

Senator Prescott seemed to be just as angry. He turned to the two bodyguards. "Go get Mrs. Prescott." After they left, he turned back to Gavin. "Who is your friend? Or should I say, your accomplice?"

Gavin stepped in front of Lacey again. "She's not involved. She just got in the way."

Lacey let that remark pass, given the circumstances. But the words stung her to the quick. Maybe Gavin really meant them, since they were so very true.

Senator Prescott gave an eloquent shrug. "But she could know things — things that might prove to be very damaging, especially if she happens to be the woman you were seen with down in the Quarter."

He looked at Lacey, waiting, but Lacey didn't speak. And she refused to remove her mask. She wouldn't give him the satisfaction of knowing she was terrified.

"Just let her go," Gavin said, stepping toward his father. Randall immediately pushed him back, the gun pointed at Gavin's nose. Lacey tried to speak, but Gavin moved to stop her, his body blocking hers. "You don't need to keep pointing that gun, Randall." Then he glared at his father. "Tell him to put it away and we'll talk."

Lacey hoped Agent Gleason heard that loud and clear.

Senator Prescott gestured and Randall

put the gun inside his jacket. Then the senator glanced over at the computer. "Did you find what you were searching for, Gavin? You know, we've been waiting for you to return. Your mother is so worried about you."

"I can imagine," Gavin said. "I'm sure she's so worried that she's had people out looking for me."

"We did track you to the Quarter, then to a town house in the Garden District," the senator replied. "Then you just disappeared. Very strange. And even more strange that you'd show up here tonight of all nights. Did you purposely hope to embarrass your poor mother?"

Gavin smiled, but Lacey saw the pain and frustration behind the smile. "My mother isn't poor or worried," he retorted. "I found the files. The secret recipe files."

The senator laughed out loud. "You broke in here to get your mother's secret recipes? I know she's notorious for her elaborate parties, but this *is* an interesting twist."

"You know which files I'm talking about," Gavin said. "The family recipes contain some very interesting figures and information — which have nothing to do with cooking, unless of course you want to call it cooking the books. I think the FBI can find a big bundle of cold, hard cash stashed in the freezer out in the pantry. Very clever."

"You're not making any sense," Prescott said, looking debonair in his black pirate costume and ruffled white shirt. He also looked nervous, Lacey reasoned, even if he was being very cautious about what he said.

"It doesn't matter," Gavin said. "It's all over now. It's too late for both of you."

"I'm afraid I don't have a clue," the senator replied, his words as smooth as silk. "All I know is that *you* seem to be the one who's corrupted this household, and *I* seem to be the one who might have to pay the price — which I don't intend to do. So I'm going to call the police and the FBI and turn you in. It's for the best, really. We'll hire the best defense team, give you all of our support. After all, you are our son."

With a growl and a sudden move that left Lacey spinning, Gavin barreled toward Senator Prescott, shoving him onto the desk. Randall tried to make a move for his gun, but Gavin was too quick. He yanked the senator around, using him as a shield. "Don't even think about it."

Before Randall could recover to turn the gun on Lacey, she lifted a crystal vase full of fresh camellias off the desk and crashed it against the man's skull. Randall went down with a grunt and a heavy thud.

Breathless, she turned to find Gavin with the senator pinned against the desk again. "I am *not* your son," Gavin said before he shoved the senator down beside the unconscious Randall. "Lacey, get the gun."

Lacey did as she was told, then handed the gun to Gavin, her nerves jolting like a live wire inside her stomach.

"C'mon," he said, dragging her to the door while he aimed the gun toward the senator. "I don't know what's keeping our backup team, but we're getting out of here." Then he told the senator, "Don't send anyone after us. I have all the information stored in a secret file of my own. And I've erased the incriminating files you planted on my behalf. By now, the FBI has the correct copies, so if anything happens to us, you'll not only be up for corruption and bribery, but murder, too."

With that, Gavin backed out the door with Lacey right beside him.

"You won't get away this time," Prescott called. "I have armed guards all around the estate."

Gavin sent the senator a chilling smile. "And I have an FBI surveillance team waiting in the wings."

Lacey received some satisfaction in seeing the senator's cold blue eyes go wide while his skin went completely white with fear.

They headed up the hallway, then Gavin pointed toward a set of swinging doors. "Take the servant hallway toward the back kitchen door," he said. "Gleason either didn't get all of that, or he's taking his sweet time getting to us. Where's Justin? I think we're going to need him."

"Parked out on the street by the front gate."

"He's our only way out of here. I left your car at another location and took a cab. And I don't trust Gleason to come to the rescue."

"I told Justin to wait," Lacey assured him. She could see the door in front of them, hear the rain pounding right along with her racing heart. They were almost free.

And then Lacey felt the wind knocked out of her as the big hand of yet another guard rammed into Gavin and caused him to fall back on her. Lacey went crashing into a Queen Anne sideboard, laden with dessert. Petits fours went flying all around her as she fell onto the polished wood hallway floor, with Gavin landing beside her.

"Well, well, the prodigal returns."

Lacey looked up at the petite, slender woman standing over them wearing a ridiculously elaborate white pompadour wig and a shimmering blue-and-white-satin bustled ball gown.

"Hello, mother," Gavin replied, sarcasm in the words.

"Gavino, you disappoint me," Nita Prescott said, her hands folded over the skirts of her ball gown. "Why do you run away? Why do you cause me so much pain?"

Lacey heard the accent, saw the flash of fire in the woman's amber eyes. And wondered how a mother could be so cold. Gavin remained silent and watchful, his eyes never leaving his mother's face.

The two men they'd seen before forced Gavin and Lacey up, but Lacey noticed the gun Gavin had before was nowhere in sight. Gavin must have hidden it in his deep pocket when they fell. That gave her some measure of confidence — that and the fierce prayer she prayed over and over in her head. *Lord, help us now.*

"Take them into the sunroom," Nita said on a hissing breath. Then she motioned to one of the men. "And go and find my husband."

After the man hurried away, Lacey saw the look in Gavin's eyes. One less guard and gun to have to deal with, she reasoned. If she knew Gavin, he was already figuring a way out of this. And she would be right behind him.

Chapter Sixteen

The sunroom was a huge long room with the same rounded doors as the drawing room on the other side of the house. Mostly glass, the room allowed a view of the lake below, and tonight, a view of the enraged storm brewing outside. The trees surrounding the house bowed and swayed, while the wind moaned and whined. Not a good night to be out, Lacey thought numbly. But Justin, bless him, was out there somewhere, waiting for her.

Gavin caught her attention, and with a slight tilt of his head indicated the doors leading out onto the long terrace. He wanted to make a run for it, she decided.

Nita closed off the doors leading to the party, then turned to face her captive audience, her bodyguard right beside her, his own menacing-looking gun at the ready. "If you had only trusted me, Gavino. We could have had it all."

Gavin inched toward one of the doors ever so carefully, then sent his mother such a harsh, penetrating look, the woman actually flinched. "I *did* trust you, Mother.

That was my first mistake."

"No, you have it all wrong," Nita said, just a shard of a plea in her words. "I planned out your life so meticulously, made sure you had the best of everything, arranged it so that you had a solid career with your father —"

"That man is not my father," Gavin said, each word an effort. "My *father* died long ago."

"*Sí,*" Nita said, her amber eyes burning with a mad brightness. "And left me here with nothing, nothing. We came to America, to New Orleans, where our relatives had made a good life for themselves. But he died —"

"And you married a rich American politician, so you could have the good life, too," Gavin retorted.

"Is that so wrong?" Nita asked. "To want better for my son?"

"No, nothing wrong in that," Gavin said. "But you got greedy, Mother. You became the middleman for all his shady dealings. You hid all the cash, you buried all the treasure. And you made a deal with the Currito family. Now you will have to be the one to face the music."

"What about family loyalty?" Nita asked. "Don't you owe us that much at least?"

"I don't owe either of you anything," Gavin replied. "You kept me at arm's length, hid everything from me. I had to find out the truth the hard way — when I was digging for information to keep *him* out of jail."

"I did that to protect you," Nita said, stepping toward Gavin. "I tried to keep you out of all of this."

Gavin nodded. "*Si*, that is until you needed someone to take the blame. You were willing to include me then, Mother. You were willing to make me the guilty party. How's that for loyalty? Did he tell you that he tried to have me killed right here in this house?"

At her surprised gasp, Gavin continued. "He sent Randall after me. Randall stabbed me with *your* letter opener. I had to leave or I'd be dead right now. But I'm going to prove what really happened. I have it all now, Mother, all the evidence I need."

Nita began to sob, the tears running down her face, causing the heavy eye makeup she wore to smear in black rivulets. "He made me do it, Gavino," his mother said, fear in every word. "I had no choice."

"You have a choice now," Gavin said.

"You can let us go and you can confess, get this over with."

By now, Gavin and Lacey were about a foot from the main door leading outside. The wind had picked up, howling its rage. Gavin kept inching toward the door, bringing Lacey along with him while the guard stood watching them. Nita held a hand up to the man and he relaxed his trigger finger.

"Are you going to turn in your own mother?" Nita asked.

Gavin made a move closer to the glass doors.

He shook his head, reached out a hand for Lacey just as the senator came through the other door. The bodyguard raised his gun toward Gavin again, while two others piled in with the senator. Outside, they heard a crash. Lacey saw a tree pop and crash to the ground down by the lake.

In that instant, Nita looked away, a great fear in her eyes. "Gavin, don't do this. He'll shoot you."

The falling tree gave Gavin just a second to pull the gun out of the deep waistcoat pocket and turn it toward the senator and his mother. "If he has me shot, he'll go to jail for murder. And so will you. If I don't shoot him first, of course."

Lacey's knees felt as if they were going to cave in, but she held her head up and faced down the bodyguards and their guns. It looked as if it would be a standoff between Gavin and them.

Nita turned to the senator. "Please, Edward, don't hurt him."

"Then tell him to drop the gun," the senator said, the words as cold and uncaring as the wind and the rain.

But Gavin held the gun higher, shielding Lacey behind his body. "I've got nothing to lose," he said, glaring at the senator. "But you stand to lose everything. Think about it."

Prescott looked uncomfortable, but he motioned for the guards to lower their weapons. "Go ahead. You won't get very far," he said on a snarl.

Gavin didn't acknowledge him. "We're leaving now, Mother. And no, I'm not going to turn you in. I have all the information I need and by now, I pray the FBI has it, too. But . . . I'm going to hope that you have enough conscience and decency left to tell the truth yourself."

With that, Gavin opened the tall rounded door to the roar of wind and rain, then started backing out with Lacey behind him.

"Gavin, no!" his mother called even as the senator motioned the bodyguards into action, their guns aimed right for Gavin.

"Shoot," the senator shouted. But Nita stepped in the way before the guards could get a good aim.

"No, no," she moaned, crying as she reached for Gavin.

The wind and rain howled, spilling cold and wet into the bright room.

And then Lacey's world shifted out of control. The senator grabbed one of the guns from the bodyguard, pushed Nita to the floor, then turned for Gavin and Lacey.

Lacey reacted purely on adrenaline and instinct by stepping around Gavin to confront the senator. "You can't do this. You wouldn't kill your own son."

"He's already said he's not my son," the senator hissed. "It would be self-defense. I have witnesses."

"Well, so does he," Lacey said, pulling off her wig and mask as she moved toward the senator even while Gavin tried to pull her back. "I am his witness. And I'm telling you right now, good will win out this time."

"Really?" Senator Prescott seemed to relax a bit, while his wife lay sobbing behind him. "We'll see about that."

He lunged for Lacey. Gavin tried to pull her away, but Prescott grabbed her and twisted her body in front of his while he held the gun to her head. "Drop your gun, Gavin. You don't want this innocent woman to get hurt, do you, son?"

Gavin looked at Lacey, a deadly fear in his eyes. "Let her go."

"Drop the gun," the senator repeated.

Lacey felt the steel near her temple, felt a hot sweat mingling with the cold wetness on her back, but refused to give in. "Gavin, don't do it. He won't kill me. As he said, there are too many witnesses. And I don't think they'd vouch for him."

Gavin glared at the man holding Lacey. Then he looked at Lacey again. "This, this is why I didn't want you here. I didn't want you to see this . . . ugliness."

She watched as he struggled with the words, then he lapsed into Spanish, tears gathering in his dark, tormented eyes. "Lacey, *mi amor. Te quiero.*"

Lacey felt the tears streaming down her own face. "I love you, too, Gavin. I love you."

Nita struggled up and stepped toward her husband. "Edward, what are you doing? You promised Gavin wouldn't get hurt. And you can't hurt this woman."

Prescott tightened his hold on Lacey and pushed the gun ever closer to her temple. "Neither of them will get hurt if he listens to me. If he will just listen to reason."

Gavin kept his eyes trained on Lacey. She could see the pain and turmoil there. And she could see something else. He did love her. She knew that now with a crystal-clear clarity. So she willed herself to be still. And she prayed.

Gavin dropped the gun. "What does this accomplish?" he asked the senator. "The FBI will find you, no matter where you go."

Senator Prescott looked around the big room, his gaze nervous and watchful. "I've always managed to elude the FBI. What makes you think anything will be different this time?" He started for the open doors, yanking Lacey in front of him.

"Let her go," Gavin said, anger coloring each word.

"I don't think so," the senator replied. "She's my insurance."

Before Gavin could respond, the wind lifted in a great moaning gust, causing several of the big square windowpanes to shatter. The senator screamed in pain as shards of glass flew right into his face. He dropped the gun and fell down to avoid the glass and debris that came with a blowing vengeance through the open door and shattered windows. The bodyguards ducked. A jagged piece of glass hit one man across the cheek. Lacey ignored the bits of glass hitting her own face, then turned and kicked the senator with her red satin pump. But Senator Prescott was holding his eyes and moaning as he lay on the floor.

Lacey raced to Gavin as a brilliant flash of lightning colored the sky. Gavin grabbed her, then pushed at the flapping door onto the terrace. The guards, worried about the senator and his wife, ignored them. The wind took the door away from its hinges in a freezing gust, then rushed at their clothes, soaking them as it threatened to blow them away.

Inside, the senator scrabbled up, blood on his face, and reached for his gun, then came running out after them. Lacey saw his eyes. He had the look of a madman, of someone who'd lost everything.

Lacey held on to Gavin, the cold rain and rushing wind taking her breath as they headed down the terraced yard toward the lake, tree limbs and debris hitting them.

They could hear Gavin's mother screaming, screaming, "No, Edward, I beg you, no!"

"Run, Lacey," Gavin shouted over the roar of the storm. "Run, baby, please run!" He pushed her out into the yard, then turned back to face the senator.

The security lights in the yard flickered, then went out. Lacey screamed. "Gavin!"

She felt Gavin's hand slipping away from hers, heard her own screams mingled with the wind and the rain as she tried to find him there in the darkness. Someone grabbed her, held her. She could hear scuffling and shouts.

She heard Justin's voice in her ear. "Lacey, let him go. The storm — I need to get you out of here."

The lights came back on, bright with biting rain and flying branches and debris.

And then she turned and saw Gavin in the sudden glare of lights out by the dock, heard him calling her name as he stood by the lake, face-to-face with Senator Prescott, the rain bashing at his clothes.

There was a gunshot and then Gavin bent double, holding his hands to his midsection as blood covered the gold brocade of his waistcoat. Lacey screamed again, the sound moving over her mind in a great echo that clashed with the hurricane winds as she broke loose from Justin and ran toward him. "Gavin, no! Gavin,

295

I'm here. I'm here."

She looked into his eyes, saw the goodness reflected there and then watched in horror as he fell back into the swirling waters of the lake.

"Why won't they search for him?" Lacey asked the question over and over, her throat raw from crying and screaming. "He might be out there, hurt. They have to find him, Justin."

Justin held her swaddled in a blanket as they sat in the kitchen. All around them, police officers and FBI agents hovered and moved. "Lacey, they're looking. But with the storm —"

"You think he's dead, don't you?"

Justin just sat there, staring at her, his green eyes bright with worry. "Here, let me wrap that blanket tighter around you. You're shivering."

"Justin," she said, speaking an effort. "Justin, I love him. He . . . he gave me this." She held up the cross necklace. "And now he might be —" She stopped, clutched a hand to her mouth. "Justin —"

"Shh," Justin said, pulling her back down in his arms. "You're safe. It's all over now."

Lacey went into his arms, the memory of

watching Gavin being swept away by the wind and the rain too much to grasp. She felt sick, so sick. She wanted to close her eyes and put the memories away for good. But the memories would never go away. Didn't she know that already?

She looked up to find Agent Gleason walking through the kitchen with Senator and Mrs. Prescott, both in handcuffs. He stopped in front of her, a big bear of a man with graying hair and dimples. "Thank you for your help, Mrs. York. Gavin —"

Lacey stood up, clutching the blanket tightly around her shoulders. "Don't talk to me about Gavin. Where were you when he needed you? He trusted you!" She lunged for the agent, but Justin held her back.

"I'm so sorry," Agent Gleason said. "The storm kept messing with our transmission signal. Gavin's voice was slipping in and out. We tried to get here as fast as we could."

"Well, you were too late." Then she turned to Gavin's mother. Nita looked haggard and drawn. She'd changed into a dark pantsuit, and her dark-brown hair fell in wet ringlets around her olive face. "And you," Lacey said, tears streaming down her face. "What kind of mother are you, anyway? You sacrificed your son — and for what? Money, power? I hope you have the decency that Gavin still saw in you. I hope you confess — at least do that to honor the son who loved you."

Nita started crying, her eyes on the necklace. "May I?" She reached out a hand.

Lacey slapped her hand away. "Get away. Gavin gave this to me. You will never get your hands on it again."

Nita began to sob. Beside her, the senator looked stoic and solemn in a dark suit and white shirt. Then Nita reached out again, her hand shaking. "Inside the locket," she said, "behind the topaz — please, there is a picture of Gavino's father. Can I please just look at it?"

Lacey's heart tumbled. A locket. Gavin had never mentioned a locket. Then she remembered his words. "This will give you the answers you seek."

Backing away from Nita and the silent senator, Lacey turned the heavy necklace over. Then she saw it. A tiny rounded compartment with a small latch. Hurriedly, she opened it, her mind racing. She knew what she'd find, and it wouldn't be a picture of Gavin's dead father.

"Agent Gleason," she said on a husky

whisper, "I think Gavin wanted *you* to have this."

Nita stepped close, then gasped as she glanced down at the folded scrap of paper Lacey handed the agent. Nita turned to the senator, a look of remorse and defeat in her amber eyes. "He was smarter than the both of us. My son was smarter than us, and *you* killed him!"

Senator Prescott shook his head. "It's not over, my dear. It was an accident. We were struggling — the gun went off. We'll get out of this. We have . . . very good lawyers."

Agent Gleason hauled the senator close. "Yeah, well, your son had some very good computer skills. He's written down the encrypted codes that connect with the rest of the bank files. This should be the missing piece of the puzzle, senator. And with everything we saw and heard tonight, and especially with that wad of cash Mrs. York told us we'd find stashed in the freezer, I'd say your political career just got blown away. With hurricane force."

Lacey closed the necklace and watched as Gavin's parents were carried away to jail. Then she turned to Justin and said, "Take me home."

The storm had passed. Her home had

been spared yet again. But not her heart, not her heart.

Lacey stood over the graves of her husband and child, silent tears tracking down her face. The cold November wind pricked at her skin, the trees looked barren and gray. And she ached with a soul-weary pain.

"Neil," she whispered, wiping at her eyes. "Neil, I loved you so much. And I loved our child. You have to know that. And then I found Gavin. I can't explain it, but I fell in love with him, too. I loved him, but it was so brief, almost like a dream. And now he's gone." She stopped, held a hand to her mouth. "I hope you can understand. And I hope that Gavin has found peace at last."

She clutched at the necklace she still wore, her mind filled with the knowledge that they had yet to find Gavin's body. She couldn't even give him a proper burial until all the red tape with the FBI was cleared away.

His parents' trial would be coming up early next year. Lacey planned to be there. Aunt Hilda had told her she needed to forgive. She owed that to Gavin's memory, her aunt had reminded her.

And so that would be Lacey's gift to the

man she'd fallen in love with. She would forgive his parents and she would visit them in prison, to minister to them. To tell them that Gavin truly did love them. And he'd wanted so badly to be loved.

"I loved you, Gavin," she said to the wind.

She turned to go home, her head down. She walked toward the grape arbor, memories assaulting her. Just as she entered the quiet retreat, she looked up to see the dark silhouette of a man standing at the other end. And she remembered seeing that same silhouette all those weeks ago, in the quietness of a great cathedral.

Her heart stopped.

"Gavin?"

It couldn't be him, of course. She was imagining things.

But he stepped closer and reached out a hand to her.

"It's me, *querida*."

Lacey gasped, then rushed into the arbor to meet him as he hurried to pull her into his arms. He had one arm in a sling underneath a black wool overcoat, but he managed to hold her close, his words cascading over her like a cleansing rain. "I promised you I'd come back."

Lacey touched his face, kissed the wetness on his golden skin. "Gavin, I love you. I wanted so much to tell you that."

"I know, I know," he said, his forehead touching hers as he stared down into her eyes. "I'm sorry. I had to get everything straightened out with the FBI. But I couldn't come back until I was completely healed."

She ran a hand over his arm, up his shoulder. "Are you all right?"

Gavin took her hand and held it to his heart. "Not my physical wounds, Lacey. But here. I had to be healed here." He lowered his head. "They were . . . my parents. My parents. I did this to them."

Lacey pulled his head down, cradling his face against hers. "And look what they did to you."

Gavin's shoulders shook with grief, but he held her there tightly to him. "I need you," he whispered, his face wet with tears. "I tried to stay away, but I couldn't find the strength. I had to come back. I had to see you."

"You're safe now," she said, lifting her mouth to his. "You're safe. God has brought you back to me."

Gavin kissed her, then held a hand to her face. "And you, my lovely Lacey, have brought me back to God." Then he told her what was in his heart. "*Mi amor.* I love you."

Lacey took him by the hand to lead him home.

Epilogue

The church bells rang as everyone poured out of the tiny Chapel in the Garden. A brilliant December sunshine beamed down through the trees, coloring everything in a golden halo of light.

Gavin turned to his bride and smiled. "We did it."

"Yes, we did," Lacey said, laughing. "But it's not over yet. Aunt Hilda has planned an elaborate reception back at the house. And it's so lovely, all decorated for Christmas."

Gavin kissed her, laughing and smiling as the well-wishers came by. "Your family likes to party."

"We have a lot to celebrate," she said, gazing up at him.

She took his breath away in her white high-necked gown. She'd come to the church riding on Lucas's big spotted stallion, and wearing a white hooded cloak over her dress, like a princess from another time. And of course she was wearing pearls — a brand-new three-strand set Gavin had given her just this morning. "To represent the three-strand cord of God's love," he'd explained as he'd placed them just over the cross necklace.

Now she was his wife.

Gavin breathed in the crisp, clean air, then gulped as he felt an exaggerated pat on his back. "Okay, I know I don't have to tell you this," Lucas said, looking dapper in his dark wool suit. "But you better be extra good to my sister, or I'll come looking for you."

"I intend to be good to her," Gavin said. Then he laughed. "And I won't be hard to find, considering your aunt has talked me into becoming a country lawyer."

"After our honeymoon in Spain," Lacey reminded him.

"She just wants you close so you can help her install that new computer system down at city hall," Lucas said with a wink. Then he turned to his own wife. "You know, suga', next to the bride, I do believe you are the prettiest woman here."

"You say that to all the bridesmaids," Willa replied, grinning over at him. She wore a sky-blue wool long-sleeved dress, simple in cut to match the looser version Lorna had worn as a very pregnant matron of honor.

"He said the same thing to me," Lorna

told her as Mick helped her down the wooden steps. "So I know he's joking."

Gavin turned to help Lorna, too. "You do look lovely. Motherhood becomes you."

Lorna nodded to Lacey. "Did I tell you how much I like your husband?"

Lacey touched a finger to Gavin's hair. "He does have a way with the ladies. And I hope he'll say the same thing when I have our first child."

Gavin grinned at her, then turned serious. "Marriage already becomes you, so I can't wait for all the rest."

Then Aunt Hilda walked up with a distinguished-looking man they all had yet to meet. Justin followed close behind with a young woman with brilliant auburn hair and stark black-framed glasses. "Who's your friend here?" Lucas asked, winking at his aunt.

"Glad you asked," Aunt Hilda replied tartly. "This is Howard Houston. I met him on my cruise to Alaska. And this is his daughter, Brandy," Aunt Hilda said, tugging the seemingly shy girl forward. "She's a botanist. Justin is going to show her around the gardens later."

Justin laughed, turned red, then smiled with a lovesick expression toward Brandy. "We have a lot in common."

"That's great," Lacey said, leaning forward to give Justin a kiss on the cheek. "She's adorable." She gave Gavin a meaningful look, then turned to Aunt Hilda's friend.

"It's good to have you both here, Mr. Houston."

"Call me Hoss," the man replied. "Everyone does."

"Welcome, Hoss," Lorna said, her expression full of mirth.

Hoss greeted everyone, his gray hair sparkling in the sunshine. "It's very good to be here on such a fine occasion."

Then Aunt Hilda placed a hand on Lacey's arm. "I'm glad you all are still here, because there is something I'd like to announce."

"What's that?" Mick asked, grinning.

"We're engaged — Hoss and me," Aunt Hilda replied, beaming. "We plan to have a spring wedding."

Lucas let out a whoop, while Lorna and Lacey gave each other surprised looks.

"Aunt Hilda, are you sure about this?" Lacey asked softly.

"Very sure," Hilda replied, leaning into her cane. "You know how it is with the Dorsettes. We tend to fall in love very quickly." She made a point of looking at

Gavin, but her smile was serene and reassuring.

Then Aunt Hilda motioned. "Let's get out of this cold. Plenty of goodies waiting at the house, and plenty of time to tell you how Hoss and I met. But before we go, I'd like to say something. Everyone, please join hands."

Everyone stilled and reached for each other, wondering what other surprises their lovable aunt had. Aunt Hilda closed her eyes.

"Dear Lord, it's been a year of storms. But we made it through and now we are all complete in Your love. Thank You for sending me three new children to love — Mick, Willa and now Gavin. And thank You for blessing Lorna and Mick with a child, and for seeing Willa and Lucas through Willa's cancer. And Lord, we especially thank You for bringing Gavin to us. We ask that You help him through the next few months as he goes through his troubles. Show him the way to forgive, Lord. Show him the way to find it in his heart to forgive his parents. We thank You for this garden — our Father's garden, that has brought all of us together. Oh, and Lord, thank You so much for Hoss. Amen."

Gavin opened his eyes, felt the tears misting there and knew he'd make it through. He'd find a way to forgive his mother and the senator. He had the love and support of this family. And he had God to guide him during the next few months of the trial.

And he had Lacey. He would always return to her, here in this quiet retreat.

He watched as Lacey's friends Josh and Kathryn helped the Babineaux clan release a pair of snow-white doves into the air to celebrate his wedding, then he held his wife close, waiting as the doves turned to fly away home.

And he felt his heart rising with them, on the wings of love.

Dear Reader,

I hope you enjoyed the last book of the IN THE GARDEN series. I'm going to miss Lorna, Lucas and Lacey and, of course, Aunt Hilda. Writing this series was both a challenge and a pleasure, but I'm glad the Dorsette siblings (and Aunt Hilda) all found love again.

The theme throughout these books has involved storms and gardens. I believe the Lord is ever present in nature. He knows when the flowers will bloom, and He knows when the rains will come. He is always there as a refuge when we have to go through the storms of life. God gives us the strength to endure the storms, if we only turn to Him in times of trouble.

My characters each had to learn this lesson. They had to depend on God to give them strength in the most trying of times. I hope these stories can help you in your own times of strife. Remember to take your troubles to the garden, where you can walk and talk with the Lord.

Until next time, may the angels watch over you always.

Lenora Worth